"I find you entrancing."

Luciano murmured, "Make no mistake about it. If you stay, you must take responsibility for encouraging me." His eyes gleamed. "I'm aroused every time I'm near you. I can't go on like that, can I? I'll be a nervous wreck," he said disarmingly.

"This is part of your ploy to make me go!" said Debbie. "Everyone can find self-control if they try," she mumbled primly, wishing she could find a little more herself.

"Not always. Sometimes—" Luciano's sculptured mouth arched sensually "—sometimes our passionate natures rebel against being held under control. That's what has happened to me, to you."

Childhood in Portsmouth, England, meant grubby knees, flying pigtails and happiness for *SARA WOOD*. Poverty drove her from typist and seaside landlady to teacher until writing finally gave her the freedom her Romany blood craved. Happily married, she has two handsome sons: Richard is married, calm, dependable, drives tankers, Simon is a roamer—silversmith, roofer, welder, always with beautiful girls. Sara lives in the Cornish countryside. Her glamorous writing life alternates with her passion for gardening, which allows her to be carefree and grubby again!

Books by Sara Wood

HARLEQUIN PRESENTS
1910—WHITE LIES
1916—SCARLET LADY
1922—AMBER'S WEDDING

SARA WOOD

A Forbidden Seduction

Harlequin Books

TORONTO • NEW YORK • LONDON
AMSTERDAM • PARIS • SYDNEY • HAMBURG
STOCKHOLM • ATHENS • TOKYO • MILAN
MADRID • WARSAW • BUDAPEST • AUCKLAND

ISBN 0-373-11952-6

A FORBIDDEN SEDUCTION

First North American Publication 1998.

Copyright © 1997 by Sara Wood.

Printed in U.S.A.

CHAPTER ONE

SABOTAGE! thought Debbie immediately. Another nail in the coffin! Anger narrowed her big, soulful grey eyes beneath her sooty lashes to nothing more than a hint of gleaming charcoal. Why did trouble come when they were least able to handle it?

'I can't believe it! *Both* Penny and Judy have left us in the lurch?' she asked incredulously.

She stalked across the kitchen floor with such vehemence that her curvaceous figure quivered with indignation and her flaxen braid swung like a bell-rope. With quick, deft movements she shed her jacket, washed her hands, and poured herself a reassuring cup of tea.

'Without the common decency to face us,' complained her mother bitterly, waving a piece of blue notepaper. 'This was stuffed in the letter-box. They've had a better offer. I ask you!'

Fuming, Debbie read the brief apology. 'It must have come after seven-thirty, when I left to take Stefano to nursery school,' she decided after a moment. 'What a blow.'

Her mother sniffed her disapproval of such disloyalty in their delivery girls and picked up the telephone receiver decisively. 'I've been ringing round for replacements. No luck so far but I'll have another go. I must say, those girls might have given us more notice.'

Debbie saw that the sniff covered up a secret despair and she wanted to throw her arms around her mother and hug away that tight, haunted look. Instead, she reached for an apron and tied it around her waist. Her mother would want the situation to be played down. East Enders were brought up to be tough, not to whine in a corner when things went wrong.

'Pen and Jude are hard up, like us, Mum,' she said with resignation. 'Who can blame them if they've had a lucrative bribe to work elsewhere?'

'I do!' grumbled her mother, dialling the next number on the list of agencies in front of her. 'It's going to be hell today!'

That could be an understatement, thought Debbie as she collected the basket of freshly baked bread. Even if they did find someone else to deliver the lunch boxes, it would take twice as long as usual. 'Try for a couple of kitchen-hands,' she suggested. 'One of us can do the deliveries.'

They were teetering on the brink again, trying not to topple into the abyss. Putting the loaves through the slicer, she reflected moodily that they couldn't keep on coping with one crisis after another. They'd met so many obstacles lately: false orders, wild-goose chases to phantom addresses, customers lost to competitors and mystifying complaints about the freshness of the food—something they prided themselves on.

'They'll ring back if they find anyone,' said her mother, replacing the receiver and sounding grim. 'In the meantime, it's action stations!'

Debbie frowned. 'I wish I hadn't hung around the nursery chatting to the mothers.' She lifted boxes of fillings from the fridge and lined them up on the counter. 'Sorry, Mum. I just like to stay till Stefano is settled.'

'Course you do, love.' Her mother picked up a large chef's knife, briskly sliced up a heap of tomatoes and slid them into a dish. 'Steffy's your priority, I've told you before.' The blade hovered uncertainly over a sweet-smelling tomato and Debbie suddenly noticed how pinched her mother's face looked. She was dreadfully worried, she thought with a sudden pang. More than the other times when they'd been in trouble. The knife resumed a fiercely concentrated bout of slicing as her mother muttered, 'He needs *one* of his parents to make him feel special.'

Debbie flushed at the dig. 'Gio adores Stefano!' she protested, struggling with her conscience and defending her ever absent husband. Gio had never hit it off with her mother. There had been a lot of rows. And his being a travelling salesman meant that he spent long, long periods away with little to show for it. Times were bad, he said. But her mother often berated him because he didn't contribute much to the family kitty.

'Steffy is a symbol of his virility and someone to play with when you're too busy,' said her mother bluntly. 'And you? Does he adore you?'

She couldn't answer that, because although her marriage was a sham she'd felt she had to keep it going for Steffy's sake. So to everyone in the family she always pretended that there was nothing wrong between herself and Gio. Despite the fact that it had virtually ended less than a year after their wedding-day. And by that time she had been pregnant and desperate to make a stable background for her child. It had been a mistake, she knew that now. And when Gio came home they'd have to talk about ending the farce.

'It's not Gio's fault that he has to work away from home so much,' she reasoned, ducking the question. But a little voice inside her said, Yes, it *is*. He could come home more often—he just didn't want to. And to be honest she preferred it that way. Her marriage had to be ended. They couldn't go on like this.

Her mother's mouth tightened. 'Your uncle offered him that job down the market. Better money, better hours. And he could have set you and Steffy up in a nice little flat instead of the one room upstairs.'

'Not now, Mum,' she begged uncomfortably. 'Don't let's quarrel over him. There's too much to do.'

The phone rang and she waited expectantly. But it was clear from her mother's gloomy expression that the agency had no one to spare.

'It's that big convention.' Her mother banged the receiver down irritably. 'Anyone who happens to have two hands has been hired. So that's it. What are we going to do?'

'Fight, of course!' said Debbie briskly. 'Come on. We're used to managing on our own.' She'd had enough practice, she thought wryly, with Gio playing a non-existent role in supporting her and Steffy. She smiled encouragingly at her mother. They'd do it. They had to.

Her mother gave a watery but unconvincing smile in return. Debbie grabbed a carving knife and controlled her frustration by thinly slicing a side of gammon while she thought how best to cope.

She was sick of hiring delivery girls and teaching them the job—the charm, perpetual smiles, the need for speed and safety combined, the low-level pleasant but persuasive selling techniques—only to have someone offer them more lucrative employment elsewhere.

This was the third time it had happened. And the sandwich business was so competitive that it would happen again and again till they couldn't stand the strain any longer. Or till her mother keeled over with the stress—like last year.

Oh, God! Debbie thought, the horror sweeping through her in waves. The memory of her mother's heart attack was still horribly vivid in her mind. Life couldn't be that cruel. Not again. Not ever again.

A sideways glance told her that her mother's hands were twisting and knotting around one another as if they might wring out the trouble from their lives as easily as squeezing water from a towel. So Debbie smiled with as much reassurance as she could muster, trying to make light of the appalling situation.

'It'll be a rush, but we can do it,' she said with commendable conviction. When faced with an almost impossible task, you just started it and kept on going till it was finished. Sounded simple, put like that. If only! 'I know this was to have been my afternoon off, but I can work all day today. You'll need help with the clearing up later. They're having a puppet show at the nursery this afternoon, so Steffy will be perfectly content.'

'We said you had to spend as much time with him as——'

'I know,' Debbie said gently. 'But this is an emergency. Steffy will be asleep half the time I'm working—he'll hardly notice. I'll call in later to tell them and give him a hug. OK?'

'Don't worry, Mum. We'll leave our oldest, most sympathetic customers till last, just in case we get dreadfully behind. Right, let's get started; customers are waiting. Better get the show on the road. Who's going to do what?' she asked bossily. 'One to cut and butter, one to dash about the City——'

'Don't look at me!' said her mother hastily. 'I'm not driving that van through central London—I haven't driven for ten years. *You've* got to be the delivery girl for today. You know you've got no choice.'

'OK, I'll do it.' Debbie flicked back her long braid with a sigh and untied her apron before checking the boxes by the door. 'Are these the first orders to go?'

'Yes, love. But you've forgotten something,' ventured her mother delicately. When Debbie looked blank, her mother grinned broadly and said, 'The costume?'

'Costume.' Very slowly, the penny dropped. 'Oh, the costume!' Two pairs of wide eyes swivelled to the froths of nonsense hanging under large polythene covers. A doubtful silence fell. Secretly appalled at the thought of wearing anything so…sweet, Debbie playfully lifted one of the dresses from its hanger and held it against her mother's skinny body. 'Suits moddom a treat,' she simpered, in the tones of an adenoidal salesgirl.

They both dissolved into laughter and soon they were clutching each other, giggling hysterically. It was better than crying, she thought, upset as she always was by her mother's fragility. It was like embracing a bony sparrow.

'No, it doesn't! I'd frighten the horses,' spluttered her mother, wiping her eyes with the corner of her apron. 'Dear Debs. You are a tonic.'

Debbie beamed with pleasure. If necessary, she'd don a red nose and do comic falls to make her mother laugh. The dress was worth wearing if it meant her mother could be left to cope in a good humour.

'Let's hope our customers think so too,' she said drily. 'I'm going to look a right idiot in this. Did I really send Penny and Judy out looking like demented Miss Muffets?' she marvelled, flicking a frivolous puff sleeve as her mother did a solemn twirl with the dress against her aproned front.

'You're exaggerating!' scolded her mother. 'It's not that bad an outfit. Rather pretty, really—sprigged muslin, and really demure. Pen and Jude loved wearing their costumes.'

'But they were drama students, Mum,' Debbie pointed out wryly.

A knot of nerves began to tie itself up in her stomach. She knew fate would have her wearing one of the costumes in a few minutes. Sprigged muslin wasn't her scene; she was too tall and big-boned and her legs were so long that the dress would hang just below her knees instead of a prim calf-length.

OK, it fitted the image of her mother's very English sandwich business—the plain, honest food, the big slabs of bread pudding, hunks of home-made pies and cakes that made City financiers' knees go weak—but would the English country girl style look ridiculous on her?

The soft, floaty skirts with masses of petticoats had looked attractive on Penny and Jude, and had brought in the punters and made people smile sentimentally on a grey London day. But she dreaded dressing up and going out on the streets of London in anything other than the inconspicuous clothes she usually wore. The delivery girls had loved their job but they were extroverts and Debbie knew she wouldn't have their chutzpah.

Torn between speed being of the essence and a sudden desire to crawl under a stone, she blinked at the pretty skirt, with its layers of stiffened broderie anglaise and taffeta petticoats beneath, and shuddered at the ghastly prospect of striding through central London looking like Bo-beep. People would stare. The knots inside her tightened.

'It's very pretty and you'll look wonderful,' said her mother with unusual firmness, affectionately tweaking Debbie's thick braid. 'You don't get out much. Good grief, you don't get out at all! About time you wore something nice and showed yourself off a bit.'

At the vote of confidence, Debbie gave her a quick but infinitely loving hug. '*Could* be fun,' she said uncertainly.

'Shut your eyes and think of England,' suggested her mother with a smile.

'I'd hit a bus!' retorted Debbie drily, slipping off her apron and dropping it on a chair. Suddenly she had a new goal in life—to find out who was trying to cut them out of business, and make them walk up and down Oxford Street in fancy dress. 'OK, let's go for it!' she cried with a light laugh. 'Give the nursery a ring for me, would you?'

With commendable enthusiasm, she scooped up both dresses and dashed into the back room of the small business premises to select whichever outfit fitted the best. At last she was able to vent her impotent anger in the violent way she dragged off her blue stretch trousers, the old blouse and baggy cardigan with its much washed and wavy hemline.

The softness that characterised her usual expression had vanished completely now. In its place was a tight, shaking fury. 'Whoever you are taking my business away,' she vowed quietly, the words shooting with soft venom through her neat white teeth, 'I'll get it back. *Every* customer. Any way I can!'

She wasn't born under the sign of Taurus for nothing. Her easygoing and loving nature hid a bull-headed determination. And she *wouldn't* let the business go under—that could kill her mother.

Money worries had a tendency to take over their whole lives till that was all they could think about. They were surviving at the moment—nothing else. Darn it! If only they were rich! They often planned what to do if they won a million pounds. She'd love her mother to stop working.

Her dove-grey eyes darkened and her plush, sweet mouth took on a stubborn strength. They'd been struggling to keep their heads above water ever since her father had died nine years ago, trapped in the cab of his lorry on the M25 after a multi-car pile-up because some idiot had fallen asleep at the wheel.

Her lovely father. How much she missed him. How much she'd longed in the lonely days of her marriage to have a husband as kind, as thoughtful, as caring and responsible. In the pock-marked mirror she caught sight of her pale-as-milk face with its charcoal-fired eyes fringed by rapidly blinking sooty lashes. Slowly she straightened, fighting the tears.

The cycle of bad luck had to end. Who cared about wearing some stupid costume when there was so much at stake? She'd go out and win more customers, she vowed, and find the chutzpah from somewhere.

With her tall and womanly body naked in all its work-honed, creamy-skinned glory, she stepped into the frilly briefs and snatched up the larger of the two outfits to slide down the zip at the back.

The material whispered over the silky gleam of her skin, giving her an alien and luxurious feeling as it glided upwards. Letting the dress sit in soft folds around her waist, she realised she'd have to dispense with her bra because the dress had been cleverly cut and boned by her aunt to lift and separate without recourse to any bra. And lift and separate it did, shaping beautifully around her generous bosom and startling her with the effect. The only mercy was that the neckline was decent, with enough broderie anglaise to hide the upper swell of her breasts. But their existence was only too plain.

Debbie blinked at the hot-cheeked woman who bore only a passing resemblance to herself. The outfit was really quite flattering; but she didn't want that because she hated people noticing her.

'Oh, boy.' she groaned, appalled to think that her figure was so clearly on display. 'I can't do it,' she muttered in growing panic.

'Debbie?' yelled her mother. 'People are demanding their orders.'

'Oh, darn!' she cursed softly. Hastily she tried on the replica eighteenth-century shoes, with their criss-cross ribbon laces and Louis heel. A bit tight, but bearable. 'I'm on my way,' she yelled back, bowing to the inevitable and fastening the huge bow of the little apron that snuggled into the sensuous dip of her waist.

'Here I am,' she cried brightly, all rustling taffeta and frothing petticoats. And despite her inner qualms she brazened it out for her mother's sake, striking a theatrical pose in the doorway. '*Voilà*! What do you think? Am I sweet and countryish?'

'You look lovely,' said her mother fondly. 'Stunning. The dress does a lot more for you than it did for Penny.'

Debbie looked down at her bosom in alarm. 'It's not too obvious, is it?' she asked anxiously.

'No. I wouldn't let you out if it were,' reassured her mother. 'You just look beautiful, darling. Except for your hair. It's all wrong.'

'Mum...oh, *Mum*!'

Debbie suffered the unpicking of the slippery silk braid and allowed her mother to tease out the rippling waves till her hair hung in a great springy fall down her back. It didn't seem very 'country girl' to her, but time was going on and she didn't dare stop to argue. Besides, it might serve to hide her face if she blushed when people stared.

A quick check of the map, then, 'Cannon Street and Cheapside, here I come,' she said cheerfully, picking up the laden baskets. 'You know where the list is for the other orders, Mum. The cakes will go in the oven at the usual time. I'll be back for the next batch of deliveries if I'm not arrested for frightening horses.' She grinned. 'Here we go. Is this going to be *fun*!'

No, she thought morosely, it's not. Dreading the coming day, she drove as close to her first delivery point as possible, parked, and hesitantly ventured out, the taffeta petticoats sounding irritatingly noisy to her sensitive ears, as if she was deliberately drawing attention to herself.

This was ridiculous, she thought grimly, suffering the double takes of several passers-by as she set off. She was having to make a spectacle of herself because some mean-minded competitor was acting sneakily. Her teeth jammed together in rage. Wait till she found out who it was—she'd grill them and serve them on toast to selected customers!

Sheer anger kept her working that morning. The journeys through the streets of London became something of a nightmare. People had seemed to think that because she was in costume she must be some footloose and fancy-free exhibitionist—despite the demure impression the outfit must have given. Soon she'd collected four invitations to dinner, three to the nearest beefburger bar and two other suggestions of the kind she'd never expected to receive now that she was a married woman—kind of married, she amended.

Remembering she was a moving advert for her business, she'd smiled sweetly and dropped a leaflet into every leering guy's car, or stuffed one into his pocket, when she'd wanted to scowl and offer knuckle sandwiches all round instead of beef and home-cured gammon. This wasn't what she wanted to do with her life!

But this was her last customer: nice old Mr Porter, one of the first people she'd ever canvassed. She smiled with joyous relief as she distributed lunch packs around the office. Slowly it dawned on her that the staff seemed tenser than at the office conference a month before, when she and her mother had done the catering. There was fear in the atmosphere. Very odd.

The lift took her to the penthouse suite. The doors slid open and she gingerly walked across the midnight-blue marble floor. Midnight-blue! Her eyes widened. Where was the beige industrial-weight carpet? Mr Porter had transformed the place!

Awed, she swept into the thickly carpeted reception-room which was luxuriously decorated in soft greens and blues, with enormous emerald and sapphire armchairs and huge displays of country flowers in shades of gold and orange. Even the paintings of autumnal English landscapes harmonised perfectly and the music in the background was sensual and seductive, smooth and easy on the ear. Stunning.

'Morning, Annie!' she said cheerfully to the secretary who was guarding the entrance to Mr Porter's office. 'I've got lunch for Mr Porter. One home-cured gammon, one smoked fish, slab of cheddar and one bread pudding. What's happened to him? The office is wonderful—and he's even changed his choice of food...'

Her voice trailed away, her surprised gaze fixed on the panelled door of the managing director's office. Hugh Porter's name had gone. In its place was a new name: Luciano Colleoni.

'That's my surname!' she cried in astonishment. 'How extraordinary. It's a remarkable coincidence; my husband doesn't have any family, you see. But what a surprise.'

'Hugh's gone!' said Annie, stating the obvious in a conspiratorial whisper.

Before Debbie could ask any questions, the intercom buzzed and an irritable and very deep, alluringly accented voice said, 'Where's my lunch, Miss Howard? It's late.'

'The delivery girl's just arrived, Mr Colleoni.'

'Send her in,' he grated in the ominous tones of a man organising a firing-squad.

Annie shot a doubtful look at Debbie's costume. So did Debbie. 'Um...I can bring your lunch in, Mr Colleoni——'

'The girl!' rasped Colleoni.

Annie raised her eyes to the ceiling. 'Don't be put off,' she whispered. 'I'm afraid he's been in a filthy mood ever since he had his post.'

'Fear no longer. I think I'm guaranteed to give him a smile,' said Debbie wryly, tweaking her pinny.

Curious to meet the new boss, she knocked on the door and walked meekly into the huge and elegantly decorated room whose buttermilk and moss-greens screamed good taste. She came to a respectful halt.

Sitting at a new and richly polished mahogany desk was a man with dark, almost blue-black hair and eyes that would cut metal. Dark eyes, like Gio's. Perhaps Sicilian, like him too—but without her husband's smooth charm and easy smile. This man didn't look as if he knew what a smile was.

Not surprisingly, perhaps, he was frowning at her appearance, the broad shoulders in the beautifully cut black pin-striped suit rising a good inch or two in what she interpreted as the weary resignation of a man who had seen it all and appeared to be reluctantly seeing it again. There was a similarly visible swell of the sharp white shirt and the royal blue tie too, and the atmosphere in the penthouse office dropped by several degrees. Oh, Lord, she thought, a man of unimpeachable taste; he didn't approve of fancy dress during office hours.

Debbie suddenly felt very self-conscious and very foolish. But she smiled her sweetest smile and approached the desk, wishing that nice Mr Porter were sitting there instead of the bad-tempered dark ogre who was eyeing her outfit as if he was afraid she'd whip out a snake and do some impromptu dance with it.

'What the hell are you supposed to be?' asked Colleoni abruptly.

Debbie swallowed the urge to giggle at his reaction. 'An olde Englishe wench, I think,' she said cheerfully. 'I had my doubts about the costume suiting me too,' she admitted with engaging honesty. His frostiness didn't dissolve by one iota as she pressed on. 'I must apologise for the late delivery...' she began, hoping to placate him.

'I said twelve-thirty.'

He radiated confidence and authority—in the way he sat, the way he commanded the room, the way he spoke, his voice very Sicilian in the way it dropped at the end

of his sentences as if he'd said something that was not
to be questioned. It made Debbie feel like a schoolgirl
who'd been hauled in front of the headmaster for some
grave misdemeanour. And she had a wicked urge to hang
her head sullenly, swing her body from side to side and
mutter, Yes sir, sorry sir; it won't happen again, sir.

But she remembered that she had to be charming at
all times and so she willed herself to approach the forbidding area between her noisily rustling skirt and the
desk. She placed the box on his pristine blotter and kept
the pleasant smile firmly in place.

'Both of our delivery girls were pinched by a rival,'
she explained calmly.

His black brow had arced up sardonically because her
cockney accent had become more pronounced—perhaps
in contrast to his classy tones, she had decided it would
be best to be herself. He'd see through any attempt she
made to sound refined.

'I'm not surprised, if they were wearing such revealing costumes.'

Debbie blinked, wondering if he'd made a joke, and
decided he was far too po-faced to do any such thing.
'By pinched I meant that our girls were lured away, given
alternative employment,' she explained, and checked
herself to see if the broderie anglaise insert had come
adrift from her bosom. All was in place. 'It's not revealing,' she protested mildly.

'It is from where I'm sitting.'

His eyes wandered critically down her body, inch by
inch, and she felt the tightness of the material increase,
proving his point.

She blushed and felt an urge to wrap her arms around
herself defensively. 'Well, it wasn't made for me.'

'I guessed.'

'You're lucky you got any food at all,' she confided. 'I've been breaking the world speed record to make sure you didn't miss out.' She beamed.

He didn't look impressed or grateful. 'The world speed record wasn't fast enough for me,' he drawled sarcastically.

'Oh. Mr Porter wouldn't have minded.'

'I'm not Mr Porter.'

'No. He was bald.' She flashed him an innocent grin to dispel his perfectly reasonable suspicion that she was sending him up. 'What's happened to him?' she asked in genuine concern. 'He's not been sacked by the board, has he?'

The man was clearly taken aback, as if people—especially Bo-Peeps in aprons—didn't normally talk to him so frankly. 'Golden handshake. I bought the bank,' he said drily.

His eyes seemed to be everywhere, appraising her with the confidence of someone who expected to be found attractive. And his arrogant gaze lingered particularly on Debbie's straining bosom. It felt hot and prickly. She was so uncomfortable that she decided she'd better leave.

'I hope Mr Porter got a good solid handshake from you,' she said, longing to find a human spark in the man. 'He was a darling. I'd like to think of him on some desert island, swigging gin and swatting flies.' The glittering black eyes hadn't even flickered. She decided to give up on him. 'Well, my feet are killing me, so I'll be off.'

'Wait.' The word was softly spoken but carried so much authority that it halted her in mid-stride as she headed for the door. And although her back was turned to him she felt his eyes burning into her spine and doing funny things to her nerves. 'I want to check the food first,' he murmured.

Stifling a groan, she returned to his desk and, carefully moving aside a stack of mail and a half-opened parcel, patiently undid the string on the box to reveal the contents. 'It's all fresh,' she said brightly. 'I baked the bread this morning.'

'You?' he said in frank disbelief, fingering a fountain-pen thoughtfully.

'At dawn,' she retorted, widening innocent eyes.

'While the mists were lifting from the Thames and the sky lightened from rose to saffron?'

Was that sarcasm? She wasn't sure—the dark face was deadpan, the eyes so intense and magnetic that she had to make a real effort to drag her gaze away. 'Not quite. While the dustmen banged about outside and next door's cat yowled in the yard,' she corrected him with a wry grin.

'Well, don't bother on my account in future,' he said, apparently not possessing a sense of humour. The hard male mouth hadn't as much as quivered in amusement. He poked about in the box, a faint curl to his upper lip. Then he looked up and met her concerned gaze with a cold, hostile stare. 'I'm re-assigning the catering to another firm.'

Debbie's mouth dropped open in astonishment. 'You're *what*? Why?' she asked in dismay. 'The food's terrific——'

'I don't have to give a reason,' he snapped irritably.

'I think you do!' she cried in protest, deciding to stick her neck out and get to the bottom of Colleoni's brush-off. 'I need to know what we've done wrong—we could put it right.'

The black eyes flashed a warning. 'I'm busy,' he said curtly. 'I don't discuss decisions.'

The strong nose had lifted with the haughtiness of a Roman emperor and Debbie suddenly felt she'd been relegated to a servant level. 'Particularly with delivery girls?' she asked quietly.

His glacial stare never wavered but she felt the scorn pouring from him like an acid river. 'Out,' he grated through perfect white teeth.

He bent his glossy head and scowled at some papers in front of him, effectively dismissing her. She was stunned. They needed the business to pay the gas bill. Her body trembled at the prospect of more debts, more arrangements to pay instalments from a rapidly diminishing income. She thought of how the news would affect her mother and steeled herself to face him, since she had nothing to lose and a lot to win. She stood her ground.

'If you're not happy with Bo-beep invading your offices, we'll deliver wearing anything you like,' she said submissively, trying to keep her voice level and mask the betraying wobble. When he raised his eyes and shot her a baleful, end-of-my-tether look, she bit her lip. 'A nice ladylike outfit.' Twin set and pearls, she almost suggested in defiant hysteria, but didn't dare.

'The costume's not the problem.'

'Isn't it?' she cried hopefully. 'Then you can't fault the food. Please let us keep you on our books,' she begged. 'We have your directors' lunch next week and food to do for the office outing next month——'

'Not any longer, you don't. Shut the door behind you.' The papers were treated to his baleful scowl again. He started crossing out whole sections of some kind of agreement, his gold fountain-pen digging hard into the thick paper and making a loud scratching noise in the silence.

Debbie was appalled at the injustice. It was so unfair! Her mouth tightened ominously. It had been a hard day and he'd made it harder. 'I won't take up any more of your valuable time. I hope you enjoy your lunch and change your mind,' she said politely, and made for the door before she lost her temper and taught him his manners.

Preoccupied with the loss of the business, she flung open the door and hurried out, her head down. There was a cry of warning from Annie and too late she saw an advancing redhead in the briefest of high-cut shorts and bra which had apparently been made from tiny scraps of the American flag. Her mind registered for a split-second that the redhead had a basket of sandwiches over her arm and then the two of them collided, collapsing on to the office floor.

'Oh, Lord!' groaned Debbie. She flicked away a mouthful of stiffly lacquered hair and made a face at the disgusting taste. 'I wish I were rich. I'd never be here,' she muttered fervently under her breath, cautiously working out which were her legs in the general jumble of limbs. 'I think,' she said tartly to the woman, 'you're trespassing on my patch.'

'*Basta*! Get up, both of you!' roared Colleoni's voice from the doorway.

With another groan of dismay, Debbie reached back to steady herself, her hand coming into contact with the frills of her briefs which were lavishly exposed to public view. Scarlet with shame, she flipped down the hated petticoats and skirt as far as she could to restore her dignity and methodically set about undoing herself from the cursing redhead. Her eyes widened in shock at the breadth and coarseness of the woman's vocabulary.

Two big male hands suddenly cupped beneath Debbie's armpits and she felt herself lifted up into the air, a light scrap of thistledown instead of a well-built mother of a two-year-old. And then she was set down on her feet again.

Her head jerked around. Level with her eyes was the unmistakable spotless white shirt and the broad knot of Colleoni's royal blue tie. Since she was above average height, she realised that he must be unusually tall but embarrassment stopped her from looking up at him.

'I wish the floor would open up and swallow me,' she muttered miserably to his tie.

'That can be arranged,' he grated grimly, stepping back as if she'd contaminate him with some foul disease.

Leaving her to squirm, he reached down and courteously helped the redhead to her feet, and was rewarded by a breathtaking display of femininity as the woman nervously clutched at the shelf that was Colleoni's broad, pin-striped shoulder. Debbie, however, wasn't mollified by the pathetic whimpering emerging from the pouting red lips.

'I want a word with her,' she said menacingly.

'Save me!' The woman cringed and clung, but didn't forget to thrust out her ample chest in a way that threatened to split the stars and stripes forever. 'Protect me,' she implored. 'That woman's mad!'

Debbie noticed that Colleoni was ignoring the redhead completely and became aware that his frowning gaze had focused with a deep concentration somewhere around her breastbone. For a moment she was riveted by the raw sexual curl of his suddenly expressive mouth and then she realised why he seemed to be breathing so heavily.

Hastily she shot a quick look down at herself and groaned at the startling amount of her own bosom that had become exposed—almost, but mercifully not quite, to the tight, hard peaks thrusting out at the sprigged material. Appalled at the way the treacherous neckline had let her down, she wriggled the modesty piece back in place again, feeling hotter and hotter as the disapproving silence deepened.

She knew she'd never get the business back now. She felt her stomach somersault with the awful realisation that her late delivery and the mortifying scene had counted against her.

Most men would have found the situation amusing—especially the ratio of flesh per metre of fabric. This guy evidently had firm ideas about women and, although he'd been red-blooded enough to spend a little while staring at her half-exposed breasts, his ideas of womanhood didn't include females who rolled around the floor dressed in fancy costumes.

'I'm not mad; I've just had enough of being sabotaged!' she said irritably, adjusting the puff sleeves and restoring some of her dignity. But not much. 'Look,' she continued sharply to Miss Stars and Stripes, 'I know it's not your fault you're working my area, but——'

'Shove off!' said the woman rudely, bending down to pick up the scattered cling-filmed sandwiches and return them to her basket. 'I'm delivering samples. Ask him. It's his sister who's got the franchise. Pia Colleoni. She's the boss of City Lights,' she sneered.

'City Lights! His *sister*?' Debbie's husky voice ran out on her.

'Sister-in-law,' corrected Colleoni. 'Leave the sandwiches,' he said disdainfully to Miss Stars and Stripes. 'I'll let you know.'

Lithe and supple, as if his muscles had been liquefied, he strolled back into his office, confident that the matter was closed. But for Debbie it wasn't; it had been City Lights which had made sneaky deliveries to some of their customers. After a moment of shocked astonishment, she sped inside after Colleoni and slammed and boldly locked the door behind her.

He froze on the way to his desk and then whirled around, his black eyes glittering with exasperation. 'Unlock that door at once and get the other side of it!' he roared. 'You're infringing my space——'

'And you're infringing my rights!' she said hotly.

He raised eloquent eyes to the ceiling. 'A woman with rights!' he said in exasperation. 'OK, now what?' he barked.

Her eyes blazed with anger. 'I think City Lights has been acting unfairly,' she said vigorously, tossing a wedge of ruffled blonde hair out of her eyes and earning herself a cynically curled lip in response.

'What are you after?' His eyebrow was making a lot of suggestions, all of them sexual.

'Justice,' she said huskily, and could have kicked herself for the breathless way that word had been delivered. She might as well have said 'sex', judging by Colleoni's expression.

He pushed back his jacket and lazily studied her while she tried to pretend that she hadn't noticed his flat stomach and the slender hips. Her brain was in a tangle and he knew that, and his menacing sexuality unnerved her utterly.

'And... how may I provide this... justice?' he asked sardonically.

She felt the wash of heat burning her face again but forged on, dragging her brain to attention. 'My mother and I are trying to run an honest business,' she said shortly. 'We provide good food at competitive prices. City Lights isn't playing fair——'

'So? That's business,' he interrupted coldly.

Exasperated, she went closer, anger and desperation overcoming her sense of intimidation.

'Sliced factory bread and soggy, chemical-injected ham don't win orders!' she said heatedly. 'They have to resort to dirty tricks: telephoning customers and saying that deliveries can't be made, undercutting with ridiculous prices and pinching staff from small businesses who are running on a shoe-string like us. It's not decent and it's not fair competition,' she stormed. 'If you won't tell your sister-in-law she's heading for trouble, then I will!'

'Don't threaten me,' he said in a deceptively soft growl that reminded her of distant thunder. 'I don't want to get involved in your nasty little squabbles. You might think it's acceptable to throw yourself at your rival delivery girls and tussle on my office floor, but I find it highly distasteful.'

She took a long, slow breath and a long, slow look at him. She sensed his claws were about to be unsheathed. Though sleek and urbane, there was something about the way he glowered at her from under his brows, the way his eyes blazed into hers, that spoke of danger. He was staring at her, unblinking, unsmiling, unmoved by her plight.

She recognised that he was more stubborn, more pigheaded than she was—with infinitely more power to hold his ground. The taut and muscled body exuded a great strength—not only a physical energy, but the sublime directness of purpose of a man who expected—no, demanded—respect and obedience. Her lashes flickered with the surprise of that discovery. She lowered her gaze in weary defeat—and found herself staring at a photograph on his desk, half concealed in some bubble-wrap as if it had just arrived in the post. It was a picture of Gio!

Startled, she rushed forward, and he flung out an arm to stop her so quickly that she lost her balance, grabbing at the nearest thing: Colleoni himself.

She was in his arms, trembling at the hardness of his jaw against her cheek and the instinctive male tightening of powerful sinew around her. Alarmed, too, by the slide of his hands up her back and the sudden warmth and silken slither of his chest against hers.

Then he was detaching himself calmly and looking down at her, his expression inscrutable. With great care, he checked his jacket for damage, shot his cuffs with a flash of gold and amber cuff-links and said tightly; 'I don't like the way you seek justice. I dislike women who use their bodies like a weapon.'

'I didn't!' she objected indignantly.

'You'll get out,' he continued, overriding her protest. '*Now*! I see you're married. What in God's name do you think you're doing, propositioning customers when they curtail contracts?'

Sick with shame, her head whirling with confusion, she ignored what he'd said and stared at the photograph in the solid silver frame, Luciano and Gio, side by side. Gio grinning, Luciano scowling. No mistake. Something lurched in her heart; Gio had said he had no family. But the photo had been taken recently—after Gio had altered his hairstyle.

She took a deep, steadying breath, her grey eyes dark with shock. Gio knew Luciano Colleoni. He'd lied to her about having no relatives. She felt her lip tremble as she wondered whether Gio had been deceiving her about anything else, and, if so, why...

CHAPTER TWO

DEBBIE felt the room whirling around. She clung to the desk, fighting for breath, and then Colleoni was forcing her head down with a none too gentle hand on her neck till she was bent over double and breathing stentoriously.

Conscious of the fact that she must present a rather provocative picture to the red-blooded Sicilian, she struggled to free herself and came up panting, her face puce with embarrassment and the effects of gravity.

'That's...'

She gulped, not from dizziness caused at the shock of discovering that her husband was linked with a wealthy financier, but from that same financier's touch. The strong hand drifted over her shoulder as it withdrew, leaving her skin alive with the sensation. Struck dumb, she struggled for a reason and decided she must be suffering from confusion. No one had ever had that effect on her—not that strong, that *intense*.

'Sit down.' When she was slow to respond, still trying to work out her extraordinary reaction, Colleoni said irritably, 'For God's sake, sit down, woman!'

'Bully,' she muttered, resentful of more than the command.

With a glint in his dark eyes, he put his firm hand on the centre of her back, unaware that he was sending more frantic signals to her brain. And, because she was dealing with the sexual messages and trying to deflect them, she offered no resistance.

So she found herself by one of the deep armchairs which faced the picture windows looking out to Tower

Bridge and the River Thames. One of the most expensive views in London, she thought hazily. And this man had bought the bank as if he'd been buying a bar of chocolate.

'Sit down,' he repeated, a little more gently. 'I'd prefer you not to faint if you can possibly avoid it,' he added drily.

She sat. And felt a lot better. 'I'll do my best,' she promised spiritedly, trying to gather her wits.

'I hesitate to suggest that your dress ought to be eased. I don't think either of us could cope with that, could we?' he drawled.

'No,' she answered hoarsely; the thought of loosening *anything* in Colleoni's presence was quite illogically unnerving. 'Oh, my feet,' she moaned, feeling them throb now that she'd sat down.

'You ought to take those shoes off. They look tight too.'

More touching! Her eyes became huge grey pools of anxiety. 'No! I'll keep them on, thanks.'

'Yes.' And he confounded her by kneeling at her feet and carefully beginning to untie the ribbon, his head close to her bare shins. 'For the sake of your comfort and your quick recovery—which I'm sure we both want,' he murmured.

In the light from the window his hair gleamed with a depth of colour like those wonderful dark plums with that faint blue tinge—the kind of invitingly glossy, smooth texture that made you reach out and... She checked her fidgeting hand quickly.

What was it about this situation that was making her feel so vulnerable? Was it the powerful and charismatic man at her feet, gently—and surely rather *slowly*—removing something she was wearing?

She gasped. Colleoni's fingers were lightly touching her ankle, nothing more, but a shudder had rippled through her body and he'd looked up, his eyes suddenly glowing with an indolent warmth.

'Something wrong?' he enquired silkily.

'I'm ticklish,' she croaked, and blushed because of the lie.

For a couple of seconds he studied her soberly while she wondered if he was reading the truth: that she found him intensely compelling; that she felt horrified that her long-denied sexual hunger was spilling out to a complete stranger.

'Really?' he drawled softly.

Miserably she watched him bend his head again and attend to the ribbons, knowing he'd recognised the signals being sent out by her body. Impatiently she waited, wondering why he was finding the laces so difficult to undo. But it gave her a chance to chill down her feelings.

She was married. Unhappily, perhaps, certainly close to divorce. But, for the moment, she was legally tied and therefore unavailable. Her body must know that, surely?

Curls of wicked, delicious pleasure wound up from her feet to her brain, touching every erogenous zone in between, and she realised that her body knew nothing of the sort and was telling her so in no uncertain fashion.

'Please...' she demurred huskily, finding it difficult to breathe.

In protest, she reached down to stop him. Their hands met, their fingers entwined. For a brief second or two they both stilled—she because of the extraordinary sensation that had shot into her chest and stomach and was now warming her thoroughly, crawling through her veins like an electric charge. It appalled her. And he—well, she didn't know why he had paused, because when his long, dark lashes lifted his eyes were big and glistening and molten but quite without expression.

He seemed filled with a vital force and his energy had flowed into her like a bursting dam filling a channel. She'd heard the expression 'a coiled spring' before but had never understood it. Now she did. It was that—the tangible force—which had disturbed her and jolted her with a few hundred volts of electric power. Nothing sexual at all, she told herself, willing it to be true.

'I'd be hard put to it to translate that plea,' he drawled, and her lips parted in dismay because she couldn't speak for the choking sensation in her throat.

His mocking, contemptuous eyes never left hers. He continued to untie the ribbons; she continued to feel disorientated and uncomfortable under the intense, mesmeric stare. With tantalising gentleness, he lifted her feet from the shoes just as her hair fell forward, brushing his face, and she felt its silken strands drifting across the flawless darkness of his skin.

And then, in a flash, he'd straightened and was standing again, leaving her flexing her released feet in relief. But she felt miserable and bemused and warily peered at his shadowed face and his husky body, which was outlined sharp and black against the glare of the sky.

But in the darkness of his face his eyes burned feverishly, causing floodgates to open within her, a terrible rush of flowing heat pouring through her veins. His energy was invading her and she was being drawn to him like a magnet and she was praying for him to have a power failure.

She had to get out. He was evil—one of those Svengali types. But she felt weak and confused, hardly able to understand what was happening to her. Because she knew, somewhere in the back of her mind, that it was nothing to do with a mere sexual vacuum that had existed within her for longer than she could remember. This was something different. Something so threatening to her vaguely ordered life and her respect for herself that she must escape.

And yet... there was the mystery of the photograph. Torn between flight and curiosity, she looked up at him helplessly, her enormous, soft eyes unknowingly begging him for help. And seeing his tense stillness, his potent and sinister stare, she grasped frantically for the banal.

'Any chance of some tea?' she asked tentatively.

A short laugh exploded from his lips as if that was the last thing he'd expected her to say. 'Tea!' The cynical mouth curled into something resembling a wry smile. 'Of course. I should have remembered the English pick-me-up, the solution to all of life's dramas,' he said a little scathingly, as if, she thought wryly, she should be knocking back double whiskies like any self-respecting Sicilian.

When he went to the desk and ordered tea over the intercom, she allowed her gaze to focus on the photograph again. Still there. Still Gio. Someone else's suit—madly elegant and expensive and so designer-labelled it would have been out of their realm—but she recognised the shirt...

She jumped. Colleoni had come up behind her so quietly that she hadn't noticed, and put a hand on her shoulder. Which she flinched from and which he drew away. But not before his wretched energy field had made her stomach contract in alarm.

'What's wrong?' he asked, coming around the chair and speaking with a huskiness that rolled through her in waves. Either she'd imagined it or he had caressed her neck with his maddeningly arousing fingers. Something had caused her skin to tingle.

Too many things were happening to her. She needed to deal with one at a time. With a shaking finger, she pointed to the photograph. 'That's...that's my husband,' she croaked.

Surprise wiped away all the sensuality, all the ruthlessness of his expression and he was briefly just plain
handsome. Seeing that she was serious, he followed her
pointing finger and then looked back at her in
astonishment.

'Impossible!' he said emphatically. 'That's my
brother—my elder brother.'

'Gio,' she persisted shakily, levering herself cautiously
to her feet.

There was a pause. 'Really?'

For a moment she thought Luciano had tensed but
when she studied him carefully she saw that he was quite
composed. She checked the photo again. It *was* Gio. Her
legs wobbled and she caught hold of the arm of the chair
as a million doubts began to wash through her mind.

'He *is* my husband.' Her bewildered eyes met his. 'He's
called Gio Colleoni,' she cried in agitation. 'I'm Debbie
Colleoni.'

And although he hadn't moved she knew that Luciano
had killed his sexual response to her stone-dead and replaced it with a wall of ice. 'You've linked our names
and jumped to a few conclusions. That can't be your
husband. I think you're mistaken,' he said coldly.

She wasn't. Her heart was pumping hard. What did
Gio get up to when he was away? Were her secret fears
right—that Gio's stories about his travels didn't ring true,
that his refusal to give her a contact number at work
was highly suspicious?

'Oh, God,' she groaned softly, closing her eyes. 'Please
let there be a good reason for this.'

'There is.' Luciano Colleoni stood between her and
her view of the photograph. 'You're mistaken. He must
be . . . similar to your husband. The photo's blurred and
there's a similarity in some faces that——'

'No. That's him,' she whispered, opening her eyes
again and staring blindly at the view. She didn't need to

look at the photo again; the image had been burned into her brain. 'That's the way he tilts his head.' She looked up at Luciano helplessly, willing him to solve the mystery. 'That's the expensive watch he won in a raffle.'

'A raffle? No. My brother bought that in Venezia— Venice,' said Luciano curtly.

'I bought him that shirt!' she cried, failing to keep her voice calm.

'There must be a million like it,' dismissed Luciano with a shrug.

'That is my husband,' she persisted in a wobbly voice. 'Heavens, we have the same surname! There aren't co-incidences like that; you must be some relative!'

'The name is common among my countrymen. If you were called Smith, would you claim kinship with any Smith who resembled your husband?'

'If there was a photograph of them both together, yes!' she declared hotly.

Colleoni strode over to his desk, studied the photo-graph and appeared to come to a decision. He picked it up and brought it over to her. 'Do you recognise his wedding-ring?' he asked abruptly.

She held the frame with trembling hands. It was evi-dently an expensive ring, a thick gold band with stones set in it. Not the cheap one she'd saved up for and which she'd exchanged with the thin band of gold he'd given her on their wedding-day.

Muddled, she looked up, her expression lost and forlorn. 'No,' she admitted.

'As I said,' murmured Luciano soothingly, taking the photograph back and dropping it rather casually on the bubble-wrap, as if it had no sentimental value to him, 'he can't be your husband. It's out of the question.'

'But... it's so like him. I thought...'

'Ah, tea,' he said, sounding relieved, as if he couldn't wait to get rid of the paranoid female making outlandish claims in his office. 'Bring it here, Annie,' he instructed coolly. 'Milk?' Debbie nodded glumly as he went through the ritual. 'Sugar?'

'Two.'

'I'll make that three.' He hesitated and then said in stilted tones, 'It must have been a shock to think that you might be related to me.'

'Yes,' she muttered, wondering if she was going crazy. But she couldn't see the photo any more. Perhaps it had been her imagination. She could be wrong.

He handed her the thin porcelain cup edged in gold and watched while she stirred and sipped, his arms folded across his brawny chest.

When she put the cup down and lifted unhappy eyes to him again, his mouth compressed as if he was stifling a wince. 'You do see that you're mistaken, don't you?' he said gruffly. 'I don't mean to be rude, but I do know my brother. I know what he would have spent on that suit, for instance, and...'

She dashed the tears from her eyes. Either he believed what he was saying and she'd mistaken the identity of the man in the photograph, or he was hiding the truth. She needed to be sure.

'It's expensive,' she said shortly. 'I take your point.'

'You're not offended?'

Luciano proffered a royal blue silk handkerchief. She gave a good blow, hoping it would wake up a few brain cells. And then she screwed the silk into a small ball in her clenched fist, her lower lip trembling with uncertainty. Maybe Gio had kept the existence of his family from her because he was ashamed of her.

Debbie swallowed the hard, choking lump in her throat, her eyes filling again. He'd made his opinions clear quite soon after their wedding-day, when he'd discovered the easy, ordinary way they lived. Gio was too smooth, too classy, his manners too impeccable for him to be comfortable in their cramped flat. Sauce bottles on the table, butter from the packet, no napkins—*napkins*!—which he'd been horrified to hear her mother calling serviettes!

And now she might be facing his brother—the elegant, autocratic Luciano, who seemed equally determined to keep her at arm's length.

'I like honest people,' she said pointedly. 'I call a spade a spade. I know my husband couldn't possibly afford to buy such an expensive suit but——'

'You...you don't have much money, then?' asked Luciano carefully, unfolding his arms and passing her a bourbon biscuit from the dainty plate.

'Not a lot,' she said cautiously, biting into it gratefully. She was suddenly starving.

'He's unemployed, your husband?'

Her eyes flicked up. 'No, he's a salesman. He's not home much. Hardly at all, lately...'

'He keeps you short of money?'

Debbie frowned and indicated that she had a mouth full of biscuit. Something in his tone spoke of disapproval—no—anger. That didn't make sense. But it was probably ignorance and he thought all men should make a fair settlement on their wives. What would a wealthy man know of budgeting? He probably gave his wife a huge allowance each month for underwear alone. If he was married.

She peered at the long, tanned fingers of his left hand which was holding out the plate again. A signet-ring on the ring-finger. But he was a Continental. She munched on the biscuit, her tongue absently lapping the thick sandwich of cream, and realised that when Luciano had pointed out his brother's wedding-ring it had been on the *right* hand, Continental style. However, Luciano didn't wear a ring on his right hand. So he could be married or he could be a bachelor.

'We're hard up,' she said defensively, wondering why her thoughts had run on so. 'Life's tough out there,' she informed him wryly.

'Is he home at the moment?' he asked casually.

Debbie shot him a quick look because there had been a thread of tension under the silk. His expression, however, was unreadable. 'Not till tomorrow. He's travelling back at the moment,' she explained, her lashes moist with slowly oozing tears as she pictured herself asking Gio for a divorce. He'd threatened to take Steffy away with him if she ever thought of leaving him. She shuddered at the thought.

'Does he call you when he's away?' asked Luciano, soft sympathy in his melting eyes.

'No.' She could explain that by saying that Gio had long since stopped bothering to call her, but didn't want to share the problems of her marriage with Luciano. She bit her lip. 'He's working in Scotland and the Midlands at the moment,' she confided. 'He's been away for three weeks...'

The dark eyes met hers with cool remoteness. 'I see. My brother lives in Sicily. He's been there for——' there was a brief hesitation '—some time.' The strong jaw clenched as though he was grinding his teeth in suppressed anger.

'Oh. It seems that I jumped to the wrong conclusion. It...it did look like him,' she said in a small voice.

'How many more deliveries do you have?' he suddenly asked.

'None. I've finished,' she answered listlessly, and gave a short laugh. 'I wouldn't be sitting here if I hadn't.'

'I'll get you a taxi.'

'No!' she cried quickly. 'I can't afford one. And,' she said as he opened his haughty mouth to speak, 'you can forget any ideas about offering to pay for one. I don't take charity. I've got my van down the road.'

'You look very pale. I don't think you should drive,' he insisted sternly.

'I'm perfectly all right.' Flustered, she slipped her feet into the shoes, only to see him cross to his desk and punch the intercom button.

'Get my driver to bring the limo to the front,' he ordered abruptly.

It sounded wonderful, but her mother would have hysterics if she turned up in a limo with a chauffeur. 'I'd rather he didn't. Thanks for the tea,' she said politely, roughly tying the ribbon laces. 'I'm grateful—and sorry to have taken up your time.'

'I'm seeing you home,' he said firmly. 'You can show my chauffeur where your van is and he'll drive it for you. No arguments,' he said, holding up his hand when she rose in protest. 'My sense of honour would be wounded if I didn't treat a lady in distress with Sicilian gallantry.'

'You *are* Sicilian, then!' she cried in astonishment. 'So's my husband.'

His mouth had tightened. 'As I said, Colleoni is a common name there,' he said stiffly.

Debbie passed a hand over her forehead, feeling she'd missed something vital. 'I'm sorry. It seemed such a coincidence...'

'Remarkable, isn't it?' he said smoothly, taking her elbow. 'Now, no arguing. Let's get you home and then I can come back and eat my lunch in peace.'

'You'll like it,' she said, allowing herself to be guided into the lift. 'It's awfully good.'

He seemed to fill the lift. The air squeezed in on her, making her breathe faster. He looked steadily at her but she studied her feet, feeling dreadfully conscious of his proximity. She squirmed irritably and heard his soft laugh.

Scowling at him from under her thick brows, she said boldly, 'Give me another chance to do your catering. Your staff don't want doughnuts and beefburgers, or plastic-tasting sandwiches. We can——'

'Family comes first,' he cut in with quiet decisiveness. 'I have promised Pia, my sister-in-law, that her franchises can supply my banks.'

'*Banks*? Plural banks?' she asked, her eyes widening.

'Plural banks,' he confirmed in amusement.

'Good grief, you must be as rich as Croesus! My statement's always in the red.'

'Things are bad, then?' he enquired thoughtfully.

'Awful,' she admitted. 'I'm not playing for the sympathy vote, but if there's a chance...'

'No. I might have to persuade my sister-in-law to re-organise her catering till it's to my satisfaction, but I will keep the promise I made. I must—you must see that.'

Debbie nodded gloomily. Their business would be wiped out if City Lights improved its food drastically and used real, fresh produce. She visualised the final nails being hammered into her coffin. Fate was kicking them both into the gutter again; she dreaded going back to her mother with the news. Her stomach sank with the lift as the floors ticked themselves off on the display unit above, not only gravity sucking away her insides, but despair too.

'Tell her to sort out her ethics as well as make improvements to the food,' she muttered, and her baleful eyes clashed with his. 'I expect no more dirty tricks from her! A fair fight——'

'Surely it can't be fair?' he pointed out as they walked out into the foyer. 'She can cut costs by buying in bulk——'

'But we can work all the hours God sends us and cook home-made stuff that knocks spots off anything produced in quantity,' she defended vigorously. 'Look,' she said, stopping in the middle of the marble floor and gazing earnestly up at him, 'get her in line. That's all I ask.'

'You think I can?' he murmured, his mouth twitching.

'You can do anything you want,' she said tartly. 'You'll always do anything you want. That's how you are. I'm right, aren't I?'

'Possibly.' The mobile mouth had softened into a smile.

'OK, well, listen.' Debbie was fighting for her livelihood now. And for her mother's health. She didn't care that people were stopping and staring, giggling, muttering behind their hands at the sight of the great Luciano talking to a gesticulating shepherdess straight out of a nursery rhyme.

She gave two back-from-lunch typists a haughty stare and returned to the matter in hand, a little surprised that Luciano was still standing there patiently, waiting for her to continue. But she had the impression that he was finding this amusing—at last. And so she'd play on that in order to get what she wanted. Justice.

'City Lights has to stop working on other people's patches,' she said firmly. 'I told you the kind of tricks they pull. My girls have turned up several times and found someone else has already delivered, having persuaded the customers that we've gone out of business. We've had staff nobbled outside our premises and offered better money. You think of a dirty trick, they've played it. It's got to stop or I'll implicate you.'

'I agree,' he said placidly.

She breathed a sigh of surprised relief. It wasn't entirely what she'd wanted. It would have been better if she'd been given the chance to continue catering for his company. However, it would do. So she treated him to a shy smile which faltered after a moment.

Luciano was looking at her oddly. It could have been admiration. It could have been anything, because she wasn't thinking straight any more. A strange, jelly-like consistency had taken up residence in her limbs, and she pressed down on her thighs in the hope that she could stop her legs trembling. He followed the movement of her hands, and then she watched in helpless fascination as his gaze made its way unhurriedly all the way up her body again till it reached her huge dove-grey eyes.

'You must have caused traffic jams right across the city,' he said softly.

Debbie floundered, lost for words. She was out of her depth with compliments like that—because, judging by the expression on his face, it *was* meant to be flattering. Was he about to make some kind of proposition? This was worrying, especially if they were going to spend time in the back of some limo.

Her aunt had said that Italians had funny morals and shocking libidos. Gio had been within earshot and had coldly reminded everyone that Italians weren't the same as Sicilians at all. But, however he identified himself, Luciano was giving out interested vibes and therefore he must be indifferent to the fact that she was married. Since he had no idea that her marriage was dead and buried, that made him immoral.

Instinctively she dragged back her tumble of blonde hair and twisted it at the nape of her neck so that it reduced his impression of a game-for-anything woman.

'I hated it,' she said truthfully. 'But I imagine my husband will be amused when he comes home tomorrow,' she added, enunciating every word carefully so that he didn't miss anything and emphasising the word 'husband'. That would tell him where she stood. 'He'll be amused to think he has a double,' she went on breezily. 'What's your brother's name?'

Luciano's eyes had narrowed. 'I don't think that matters now,' he said quickly, and drew her firmly out to the waiting car. 'And ... I'd prefer it if you didn't tell your husband about meeting me.'

Debbie flushed. 'He won't try to sting you for a loan on the basis of sharing a surname, if that's what you're worried about,' she said, bristling at his stiff request. He neither confirmed nor denied her assumption, and she slipped a little huffily into the passenger seat of the elegant Bentley.

There was a silence on the way back. Wrapped in some beautiful orchestral music that was probably classical, she leaned back in the seat and enjoyed the ride. He drove with a heavy, preoccupied air that didn't encourage idle chit-chat and she, for once, was relieved to be quiet. Occasionally she glanced at the brooding Luciano and wondered how she could ever have imagined that Gio might have been his brother.

The two men were so different. Luciano vibrated with power and that fascinating, disconcerting energy, whereas Gio was ... She flushed, hating the truth. When he *was* home, he lounged around expecting her to fetch and carry for him, even though she was working from dawn to midnight.

If he were driving now, Gio would be lounging with one hand out of the window. He'd be more reckless, too, and he wouldn't have stopped for that party of schoolchildren or waited so patiently for the old woman to teeter over the crossing. He certainly wouldn't have jumped out of the car and helped her to pick up the potatoes that had spilled out of her basket.

It had been a very revealing action on Luciano's part. She eyed his hands, now grubby from the soil on the potatoes, and knew that Gio would have cursed the old woman for being a nuisance, perhaps shouting a clever remark out of the window before driving on.

Her teeth dug into her lower lip, hating the way her thoughts were going but incapable of denying the truth.

'Do you see your brother often?' she ventured, hoping to banish all the uncharitable thoughts from her mind.

'Not much,' he said flatly, and she got the impression that it was no great loss. Perhaps that explained his casual treatment of the photograph—and his scowl. 'He lives in the north-east of Sicily, I work in London.' He switched the direction of the conversation smoothly. 'Your premises are near Guy's Hospital, you said?'

'Yes.' He seemed to know his way around London very well. 'If your sister-in-law runs City Lights, she must spend a lot of time apart from your brother,' she mused.

He gave her a quick, startled look. 'Half running it,' he corrected her. 'She inherited the franchises from her father. He still controls the business on a day-to-day basis while she handles the marketing strategies and acts as a sort of ideas woman. So she does a lot of business via computer link from Sicily and spends a lot of time commuting between Palermo and London. Well, she's been doing that for the last few months or so. I'm surprised at her interest. She never cared to work before—now she's obsessed with it. Usually Gio comes to England with her and visits... friends.'

Debbie froze. 'Gio. You said Gio!' she cried, turning accusing eyes on him.

'Did I?' Luciano sounded a little too surprised and Debbie felt a cold hand clutching at her stomach. 'How extraordinary,' he said with a light laugh. 'Must have been your saying the name so often.'

'What *is* your brother's name?' she probed with quiet determination.

'Valentino,' he answered glibly. 'Don't pursue it any further,' he advised tightly, his profile grim and forbidding. 'Don't pursue it,' he repeated softly, like a litany, as they drew up outside her premises.

He peered at the shabby shop, once a newsagent's, its window whitewashed to give them privacy inside while they cooked and dashed around preparing orders. 'Is this it?'

Debbie wanted to explain that it was all they could afford, that there was living accommodation above, that the kitchens were sparklingly clean and they produced miracles inside. But she kept her mouth shut about those things.

'Yes. Thank you.'

The van, which had been following close behind all the way, drew up behind them and the chauffeur struggled with the bent door. Debbie went over and gave it a bang in the right place, grinned at the man as it flew open, and went to the back of the van to collect the empty baskets.

Luciano was standing at the pavement, frowning at the peeling paint on the shop-front as if it offended him. She was about to thank him again, when her mother appeared in the doorway.

'Debs?' she asked uncertainly, her eyes switching from the chauffeur to the elegant Luciano and his glorious mirror-polished car, all of which looked extremely incongruous in the run-down little street. 'Nothing wrong?'

'It's a long story, Mum,' she said with a reassuring smile.

'Mrs...?' Luciano held out his hand politely.

'Baker. Stella Baker,' said her mother, wiping her sudsy hands on her pinny.

'Luciano...' He smiled so engagingly that her mother lost her uncertainty and shook the proffered hand warmly. 'Luciano,' he said again, with a small flicker of his eyes in Debbie's direction as he deliberately omitted his surname. 'Your daughter felt a little unwell,' he explained. 'I believe she'd been working flat out without anything to eat. Since I was coming this way,' he lied easily, 'I said I'd drop her here.'

'Well!' Her mother beamed and patted his arm. 'You're all right, you are. Thanks a lot.' To Debbie's dismay, her mother leaned her sparrow-like frame closer to Luciano and muttered, 'Debs works twice as hard as she ought to because she thinks I'm going to fall down dead if she doesn't. I keep telling her I'm a tough old woman.'

'Hardly old, I think, Mrs Baker,' demurred Luciano. 'Let's see... your daughter must be in her late teens, so you are...' he dropped his voice, as if her age were a state secret '... late thirties? Married young? Perhaps——'

'Oh, please!' Her mother blushed.

Debbie's mouth opened in amazement. When Gio had tried similar flattery before they'd married, her mother had brushed him off impatiently and said he was too smooth by half. Luciano was a better flatterer; he actually sounded as if he believed what he said.

And she, in her late teens! She tried to keep back the giggle. He'd get a shock if he knew she was twenty-five!

'We've got a lot of washing-up to do. Greasy pans. Sausages to make,' she said prosaically. 'Me and the youngster here,' she added straight-faced, indicating her mother, who put her arm around Debbie's waist and gave her a hug.

'Thanks for bringing her home,' Stella said to Luciano. She smiled affectionately at Debbie, whose eyes instantly glowed with the warmth of love. 'She means the world to me.'

There was some emotion tugging at Luciano's mouth and it seemed to Debbie that he didn't know whether to smile or be sad. Puzzled, she gave her mother a quick hug back and watched him carefully.

'There are people who would give the world to have what you have,' he said gravely to them both.

'Yes, we're very lucky,' Debbie acknowledged quietly.

He hesitated as if he wanted to tell her something and then frowned and lowered his thick fringe of black lashes. Debbie felt a little pang eating into her heart because he would go now and they'd never meet again. Perhaps it was just as well—he seemed a very dangerous man to know.

'I hope your fortunes improve,' he said with deep sincerity and then he turned, got back into the car and was driven away, his eyes rigidly fixed on the chauffeur's head.

Debbie stood mutely on the pavement and then followed her mother in, knowing that she'd have to explain what had happened, and that she'd leave most of the important stuff out; otherwise her mother would read all the right things into the extraordinary attraction she'd felt for the worryingly magnetic Luciano.

She delayed answering her mother's barrage of questions by protesting that she had to change out of the outfit first. In the privacy of the little back room she stared at herself, amazed to see that she didn't look any different.

She felt different. Despite all her endeavours to remain indifferent to Luciano, she had secretly coveted him—a virtual stranger—and felt a stir of sexual energy so strong that she was fully aware that it had the potential to be more powerful than anything she'd ever known. It was frightening.

Today she'd met someone who'd shaken her world.

The next day, Gio didn't come home at the expected time. When she found herself fretting at the fact that she couldn't finish her farce of a marriage—yet feeling a sense of utter relief at her freedom from her husband's oppressive demands—she knew that seeking a divorce was the right decision. There was no marriage any more. There hadn't been anything between them for a long while and they both knew it. It was time to tell her mother the truth.

A great weight seemed to lift from her shoulders. It seemed obvious now that her extraordinary response to Luciano had been a symptom of her need for liberty. A kind of rebellion, a 'hey, I'm alive!' kind of protest. That was why, she reasoned, trying to explain her alarmingly powerful feelings, she'd thought of nothing but Luciano since meeting him. And, of course, it was understandable, wasn't it? He was drop-dead gorgeous and he'd got physically closer to her than any man for a long time.

Finding him impossible to shake from her mind wasn't a crime. He'd have had that impact on any woman. She'd been vulnerable and it was no wonder that she'd been incapable of warding off the extraordinary chemical bombshell that had hit her when she'd been within ten yards of Luciano Colleoni.

But it annoyed her that, whenever she thought of Luciano, her heart fluttered like a pigeon's wings and her body fired up as if he were still watching her with those flame-thrower eyes. Oh, Lord, she sighed as she dropped yet another plate from her nervous fingers, the man's costing me a fortune!

Time and back-achingly hard work successfully banished anything but practicalities from her mind. Her mother had found two student replacements to make the deliveries and she remained in the kitchen all day.

In the late evening, she lovingly tucked her son up in bed, giving him a specially long cuddle. For a moment she gazed down on him, his dark brown spaniel's eyes now closed, the heavy girlish lashes still at last on his honey-coloured cheeks. Her hand gently stroked his hair, which was as blond as hers, and then she sighed with pleasure and went off to set the baking-trays ready for her dawn start.

'Just going downstairs, Mum!' she called in the direction of the small living-room.

'OK. I'll listen out for Steffy.'

Debbie smiled to herself, knowing that her mother would tiptoe in and stare at her beloved grandson for a few private minutes. He was as precious as the crown jewels to both of them. Sometimes Debbie became so overwhelmed with the emotion she felt for her son that she could imagine fighting to the death to protect him from harm.

Thinking of his sweet little smile and the chubby little elbows and knees she'd just nuzzled, she slipped down the back stairs to the kitchen, flicking a switch that bathed the big room in cold, artificial light.

Halfway through the routine of preparation, she heard the purring of a car's engine—unusual because anything around her street normally had a faulty exhaust or pinked a bit. And then, when the authoritative knock came on the door, she knew who it was.

Luciano.

Rooted to the spot, she stared with wide, panic-stricken eyes at the unmistakable shape of his magnificent body through the frosted-glass door. She could pretend no one was here. She ought to, for her own sake. Already she felt the nervous fluttering of her pulses. But he'd only come back again; he was that sort. And why was he calling, anyway? He knew her husband was supposed to be with her so it couldn't be in the hope of some romancing on the side.

He knocked again, more sharply. Not wanting her mother to hear, anxious to keep his call a secret, she ran to the door, conscious as she did that she was wearing old clothes and no make-up. Vanity made her groan and then she let her soft mouth curve into a rueful grin. What a contrast to the outfit he'd last seen her in. At least he'd see her as she really was.

'Oh, it's you,' she said, simulating cool surprise.

He looked drawn and tired and was dressed in a severe black suit with a black brocade tie. Her pulses immediately began to accelerate at the sheer intensity of his innate masculinity.

'I want to talk to you,' he said curtly, his eyes smoky with exhaustion.

'Oh.' She wanted to console him, to ask what was wrong. It worried her that she felt that way.

'Will you ask me in?'

'I...I don't think so,' she said.

He took a deep, deep breath and her hand went involuntarily to her breast because whatever he was projecting at her—knowingly or unknowingly—it was dangerous and should have carried a health warning.

Luciano gave her a jaundiced look. 'Is your husband in?'

A lie. It would be wiser...or else he'd push his way in, look at her with those damnably sexy eyes and... 'Yes,' she said, aiming for joy, but the untruth stuck in her throat and her answer came out huskily.

'I see. Then that's all right. If he hadn't come home——' He cut himself short. 'I'll go.'

She watched him turn and felt prickles of foreboding running up and down her rigid spine. If Gio hadn't come home...what? Curiosity—and some dreadful premonition—made her call out. 'Wait!' she cried urgently.

Over his shoulder, his eyes mocked the very idea of doing so, as if he knew it would be wiser to keep his distance. 'I think I'd better not,' he drawled. 'Don't you?'

He knew. His mouth, those knowing eyes told her that he was perfectly aware of what she was feeling—that he disconcerted her and set her nerves on edge. Debbie swallowed, knowing that wasn't the whole truth. She licked her lips carefully like a cat and he let his gaze flicker down to her moist mouth.

Then he turned away, waiting patiently for her answer but staring doggedly into space. So she spoke to his broad back, some terrible urge making her want to touch the beautiful soft cloth and feel the tense, touchable muscles beneath. Aghast at her slipping senses, she made her tone sharp.

'My mother's in. But...look, I was lying; my husband hasn't come home. I don't know where he is. You said "If he hadn't come home". Why would that matter?' It was something to do with the fact that both men were called Colleoni. She knew it. Her mouth trembled. 'Why do you want to know about him?' she asked in a quick, breathless tumble of words.

The shoulders had slumped. And then he slowly came to face her. 'So he hasn't returned. I was afraid he hadn't,' he said quietly. '*Hell*!' He stared at her in perplexity as if he didn't know what to do next and found the experience alien to him. 'I'd hoped... God, this is a mess. Why did you lie?' he barked.

Debbie hung her head. 'I'm busy,' she said, frowning at her scuffed shoes. 'I didn't want...I didn't want to be bothered.'

'This is important,' he told her grimly. 'If your husband hasn't come home I must speak to you and you must give me time to do so. You'll need some privacy for what I have to say and you won't want to hear it out on the street, I can assure you.'

She swallowed nervously. He wasn't feeding her a line; it was something serious—something that concerned Gio. And it was something unpleasant. Apprehensively she pushed open the door and moved back, inviting him in, her eyes huge with anxiety.

CHAPTER THREE

DEBBIE took a steadying breath. 'I—I'll call Mum.'

'No,' Luciano said steadily, ice in his eyes. 'Don't bring her into this yet.'

'Into what? What is it?' she half whispered as he stepped inside. 'What is it? Something's wrong, isn't it? What do you know?' Nervously she clutched her hands together, wringing them as her mother did, squeezing till the flesh hurt. Luciano's face was so grave and he looked so...pitying... 'It's Gio, isn't it?' she said huskily. 'You know something about him. *What*?'

'Sit down.' A strong hand forced her into a hard-backed chair and then Luciano flexed his knees and hunkered down to her level, pinning her frantic eyes with his piercing dark gaze. 'You're right. I have come to tell you about Gio,' he said softly, putting a hand on hers where they twisted in her lap.

Stillness overtook her. 'Yes, go on,' she mouthed, her pale face whitening like chalk.

He knew things about him, things she perhaps didn't want to hear. She could tell him to go, clap her hands over her ears and not listen, and then Stefano's life would be untouched by scandal or recrimination or...

'I'm sorry,' Luciano said in a low tone, his eyes bleak and pained, 'but there's been an accident.'

Her hand flew to her mouth to stop the involuntary cry that might have alerted her mother. Over her fingers she blinked at him several times as if Luciano might vanish and prove to be a figment of her imagination. But he was still there, steady and solid like a dark rock,

51

and she knew he was ready to support her if she needed him. That fact gave her an irrational comfort and the strength to rally her self-control.

'An accident! Tell me,' she rasped, not wanting to ask the obvious question, Is he alive? 'Who—who is he to you?'

'My brother.' He waited for some reaction, perhaps anger or a barrage of questions, but she felt numb.

'Brother,' she repeated dully, willing him to continue.

He saw blank incomprehension in her huge slaty eyes and winced, then bowed his head briefly and continued in his rich, deep voice. 'Apparently he was driving on a mountain road in Sicily. There was luggage in the back of his car and a ticket—Palermo to London...'

'He was coming home,' she said with a frown. He was dead, she knew it by Luciano's tone, his solemn manner.

'Yes,' Luciano said huskily, 'And, perhaps eager to catch the plane, he took a bend too fast and the car went over the edge.'

'And?' she prompted quietly.

There was a tenderness in his eyes that confirmed the answer before he spoke and prepared her a little. 'It landed a thousand feet down. His neck was broken instantly and I'm assured that he suffered no pain...'

'No pain,' she echoed flatly. Luciano flinched as if he had lived that moment of his brother's death many times since early that morning. 'Oh, Gio...' she said with an immense sadness. He'd wasted his life with her. He could have been happy with someone else—and she too. 'He was so handsome,' she mused bleakly, remembering his pride in the way he'd looked. 'His face—was it...?' She covered her own face with her hands. It was awful. A terrible way to die for someone so young.

'I'm told he looks as if he's at peace.'

'Peace?' Gio had never seemed content when he was alive. How ironic.

Luciano drew in a laboured breath, pain etched into every line of his face. Her soft heart made her long to console him but dared not. If she fell into his arms and cried, she knew that that action would bind them together in some strange way. And so she used every ounce of her energy to keep herself rigid and unresponsive.

'I'm sorry to bring this news to you.' He took her icy, limp hands in his and began to massage them with an absent-minded gentleness. 'It's an awful thing to hear from a total stranger. I wish... I wish he were here, safe with you.'

All she felt was a heavy paralysis as if she'd been anaesthetised. No emotion. Nothing. Gio was dead and yet she felt as if he had never been a part of her. That made her feel guilty—and yet it was the truth. They had been virtual strangers. It had been an odd marriage. When Gio had been away, she and her mother and Steffy had lived in their usual independent way, she and Stella working without pause from early morning to late at night. At weekends they had scrubbed out the kitchens, planned menus and done the books.

On the rare occasions when Gio had been home, she had had to creep out of bed even earlier to get things done. He had wanted her life to revolve around him. It was like being on two different planets; first he'd be tired and spend his time lounging around, issuing petulant requests for attention, and then he'd want her to drop her work and go out with him to expensive clubs that they couldn't afford, though he had always seemed to have money to spend.

It had saddened her that they'd never talked. Not about important things. Like what he had been like as a little boy. She blinked. Gio had never told her anything about himself. 'Live for now!' he'd cried when she'd tried to delve, longing to know everything about him. Perhaps he hadn't wanted her to find out about his

wealthy brother. Perhaps he had been ashamed that he'd
not made his fortune too.

Miserably, she realised that Gio had died and she
hadn't really known him. Stefano would grow up and
she wouldn't be able to tell him much about his father.
Not his hopes for the future, his aims or ambitions. Only
superficial things.

Was that why she felt nothing but a vague sadness?
She and Gio had never been friends—and hardly lovers—
after their first year together. A terrible emptiness swept
over her. Gio hadn't trusted her enough to confide in
her and she felt cheated, as if she'd been locked out of
a significant part of his life. There must have been so
many lies. Luciano had lied to her too.

'You said your brother's name was Valentino,' she reminded him resentfully, glowering even though the lie
made no difference now.

'Gio Valentino Colleoni. I lied because . . . I felt it was
none of my business what my brother chose to reveal to
you,' he said carefully.

She lifted her head and met his patient gaze. He was
suffering. The pain of hell was written on his face. It
was as if every inch of his flesh had been compressed
by the tensing muscles and drawn across his angular
cheekbones. Her hand lifted from his grip to touch his
face in sympathy and then she let it drop again. It was
immediately captured in his comforting grasp.

'Why didn't you want me to pursue the idea that we
might be related?' she asked shakily.

'Gio obviously had his reasons,' he answered
awkwardly.

'I think I know why,' she said listlessly. 'He was
ashamed of me and my family.'

'He had no reason to be ashamed of you,' Luciano
said with a throaty softness that eased her distress a little.

'I know he was.' She took a deep breath. 'This must have been difficult for you, coming here.'

'It was my duty to tell you.'

'Thank you,' she muttered gratefully. She passed a shaking hand over her forehead, sweeping back the wisps of hair that had escaped her plait. Nothing was happening in her head. She thought, Poor Gio, but the emotion seemed blocked. Maybe it would come. He'd been her husband, after all. She was in shock and it hadn't sunk in. Luciano's tension seemed more real to her. She looked at him with compassion. 'He was your brother,' she said huskily. 'You must be so upset . . . Can I get you a drink or something?'

'Me?' Luciano frowned as if he hadn't considered himself at all. 'That's not important.' He hesitated. 'We were virtually estranged,' he told her uncomfortably. 'We only met a couple of times last year and quarrelled on both occasions. I saw him a month or so ago and——'

'When the photo was taken?'

'Yes. A street photographer took it. Gio sent it to me as a reminder of our acrimonious meeting, I think. That's why I was in a bad temper the day you walked into my office,' he admitted. 'Just before that photograph was taken we'd had a violent disagreement about . . . his way of life.'

'His job, you mean? Or . . . did you know he was married to me and you objected to that?' she asked, tensely awaiting his answer.

Luciano frowned at his signet-ring and eased it on his finger. 'I didn't like what he did,' he said eventually, 'and I knew he . . . I was aware that there was a woman he visited regularly.'

'I feel as if he kept me a secret so that his family never had to meet me!' she said with sudden vehemence. 'I resent that.' She resented a lot more. Her mouth tightened. How could he have done that to her?

'I understand your anger,' Luciano growled. 'I didn't like his cloak-and-dagger secrecy either. I asked him who he was visiting, if it was serious...'

'That's why you wanted to know if he was looking after me.' Her eyes softened with warmth. Luciano had wanted to act honourably and he'd been upset when he'd seen how his sister-in-law was living. 'Did he tell you about me?' she asked curiously.

'No, nothing. He said there was no one special,' said Luciano bitterly. At her gasp and the hurt expression on her face he squeezed her hands sympathetically. 'I accused him of lying and asked him to consider settling down. The note with the photo made it clear that he wanted me to go to hell. I was going to dump the photo in the bin.'

'You didn't get on. How sad.'

She studied his unhappy face and felt the urge to take him in her arms and hold him and tell him that he mustn't regret his inability to like Gio. But she knew she'd blurt out the truth—that his brother had been selfish and thoughtless and rather unpleasant at times—and she couldn't hurt Luciano. He looked so shattered. Blood was a very strong link, she thought. Stronger than marriage.

'We only ever met to discuss family business,' he said quietly. 'Whereas you...' He lifted a finger and stroked her soft cheek thoughtfully. 'It must be more of a shock for you.'

She wondered what he must be thinking, whether he thought less of her for not weeping and wailing. If only she could. It would get rid of the hole where her emotions should be. In films people gasped and sank to the floor or fainted. All she could do was to sit there dumbly and wish she'd given up on the marriage earlier, for both their sakes.

Seeing that Luciano was waiting for some kind of response, she made a big effort to speak. 'I don't feel anything,' she told him honestly, her eyes huge with guilt.

'No; I didn't at first,' he said, reassuring her with a kindness that made her feel even more guilty. 'I barked out a lot of questions and started making arrangements. My mother must have thought I was a callous so-and-so.'

His mother. Debbie felt a bitter sense of regret. Stefano had another grandmother who knew nothing of his existence. Why? What family row had broken all the ties to such a dramatic extent? Gio had told her that he was alone in the world. He'd lied. And she feared the existence of other lies.

Something else niggled in the back of her fuddled mind—something important, a piece of a jigsaw that wasn't fitting. Try as she might, she couldn't bring it to mind.

'I'm normally emotional. I'd prefer to cry,' she said huskily, drawing her hands from his and picking at her threadbare cardigan with embarrassed fingers.

'You're bound to grieve later, when you realise what's happened,' said Luciano quietly. 'At the moment I suppose you're still digesting the fact that I am your brother-in-law.'

The idea shocked her. It seemed a suddenly intimate relationship to have with the worryingly compassionate Luciano. His surprising warmth and genuine concern were turning her original opinion of him upside-down. Whatever his distress, he seemed more anxious to comfort her—but then he didn't know that she hadn't loved Gio and she couldn't tell him, not right now. He'd be too upset that she'd prevented Gio from finding happiness elsewhere.

'It takes some getting used to,' she admitted.

'For me too. I knew before you did and yet I'm still making the adjustment,' he said with a frown.

'I can imagine your shock when I turned up at your office and you realised who I was,' she ventured.

'More of a shock than you know,' he said grimly. 'Look, I imagine you have a lot of questions about Gio and about us, his family. Fire away. Ask what you want.'

She turned her head away. 'I—I'm not sure I want to know,' she muttered jerkily. The elusive fact which she wanted to retrieve was something to do with the family. A fact she ought to remember . . .

'That's your choice.'

Numbly she nodded and heaved a deep sigh. Luciano's eyes were on her still, watching every emotion that flickered over her bemused face. She knew he was waiting for her to ask questions yet somehow Gio's past didn't seem important any more—only that he hadn't shared it with her.

But she managed one. 'When is the funeral?'

Luciano gave a quick frown and became engrossed in studying her hands, which were still twisting in her lap, pulling at the knitted cardigan. 'Ten days from now. It's taking place in Sicily, of course. It's had to be delayed for a while—police formalities—and so that our far-flung family can gather from various parts of the world.'

He raised his eyes to hers and they were veiled. She knew instantly that he was hiding something from her and her fingers became more agitated than ever till he put his hand on them and made them lie still. But they trembled. He was pouring his energy into her again, giving her strength.

'Ten days,' she repeated dully.

'You're deeply shocked, I can see that,' he husked. 'I can arrange for someone to stand in for you, to do some cooking or deliveries. You tell me whatever help you need and I'll organise it so that you can visit a church here on the day of his funeral.'

'Here? Why should I want to go to church here? I'll be going to Sicily!' she cried in astonishment.

There was a quick dipping of his black brows. 'You have too much work, surely? And the expense...'

'Work? My work can go hang,' she said in agitation. 'What do you think I am? He was my husband—I have to be at his funeral.'

'I think you would be upset,' he said flatly.

'Yes, no doubt I will be,' she snapped, flushing because she was still deceiving him about her feelings. 'That's what happens when people go to funerals—close relatives get upset. Is that any reason to duck out?'

'It's a long way. Flights could be difficult to get and you'd pay over the odds,' he said plausibly. 'And then how would you get from the airport to a remote country village?'

'I can drive,' she retorted edgily, mystified by his insistence that she was incapable of coping in a crisis, and a little offended that he hadn't suggested that someone in the family might help her out.

'Sicily isn't like England,' he told her with an astonishing display of irritability. 'I strongly advise you against it. Palermo traffic is impossible. You can have no idea how foul it is till you go.'

Debbie frowned. This was crazy. 'Then I'll find out,' she said sharply. 'I'm not feeble. I'm going; I can borrow the money from my uncle and pay it back.' Her defiance was short-lived and it withered when she thought of the journey ahead. 'I know it'll be awful, but I have to go,' she said, her gentle mouth quivering. 'Surely you can't deny me that? I have a right...'

'So,' he muttered grimly. 'You've made your mind up. I can't persuade you of the wisdom of staying here in England.' It was a statement rather than a question, as if he had realised she wouldn't dream of changing her mind.

Pale and unhappy, she met the hooded black eyes and said with quiet determination, 'No, you can't. I will go. I must.'

He swore under his breath and then nodded his dark head slowly, as if he'd suspected as much all along. 'You'll regret it.'

'How could I?' she asked passionately.

'You'll find out,' he said.

And suddenly she realised why he would prefer her to stay in England. 'You don't want me there,' she accused shakily. 'You with your elegant suits and city grooming. You hear my accent and you think I'm common. You look at me in these cheap mail-order clothes and you cringe and think I'll embarrass your family and friends——'

'God, no!' he interrupted forcibly, the words almost exploding from his mouth. 'Your clothes are the least of your problems.'

Her eyes widened warily. 'What do you mean?' she demanded, her heart pounding with nameless terrors.

Debt? Had Gio owed his brother money? Would she have to pay it back? She shuddered to think of herself in Luciano's power, owing him favours.

He drew in a long, resigned breath. 'I suppose you have to know,' he said ominously. 'When I tell you, I think it would be better if you were somewhere else instead of here. Your mother might come down and interrupt us and you'll want time to choose your words carefully when you speak to her.' His mouth was grim. 'You may even want to keep the information to yourself.'

'That sounds terrible,' she whispered. Her pounding heart missed a beat. A truth. Luciano knew some awful truth. More secrets. She began to tremble. 'Is he dreadfully in debt?' she breathed.

'Not as far as I know.' Luciano studied her with a hint of compassion in his searching eyes. 'It's a little more delicate and personal,' he said gruffly. 'Can you get away from here?'

Apprehension was breaking her rigid control, making her quake with fear of the unknown. She racked her brains for that elusive piece of the jigsaw. Nothing came to mind but she *knew* she ought to have it close at hand. It was so frustrating.

'I don't know...I'm not sure what to do. I need time...I haven't taken it in... Oh, God,' she whispered, rambling on as if Luciano weren't there. 'I'm in such a muddle. I don't...' With an urgent gesture he touched her knee, reminding her of his question. 'Luciano, what do I do? Shall I tell Mother now about Gio being dead and explain that's why I'm going out? What's going to happen to me? Is something awful in store? You must tell me now! How do I——?'

'Wait!' Luciano's rapped-out command halted her incoherent meandering and brought her up sharp. 'Your mother's upstairs?' She nodded dumbly. 'I'll handle this. Don't move,' he ordered.

As if she could, without help. Complete apathy had claimed her body and her mind. For the moment, it was all she could do to stay upright in the chair. Her brain seemed to have gone into a state of shock as if it was waiting for Luciano to release it and set it working again with the threatened revelation.

Trembling, and staring into a black void where the homely kitchen should have been, she heard Luciano walking up the stairs and calling in a polite, almost tentative way to her mother, heard the happy answer that told her he'd been fondly remembered, and listened while he explained that they were going out for a quick drink to discuss an urgent catering job.

An easy lie. She shivered. Were both the Colleoni brothers practised liars?

Luciano hurried down the stairs and her mother called out, 'You'll be OK, Debs?' just as a precaution.

Making a superhuman effort, she arranged her vocal cords and shouted back. 'Course, Mum!'

'Take a piece of that apple pie, dear, and give him a taste,' cried her mother cheerily. 'That'll clinch any deal.'

Luciano looked at her as she sat trembling on the chair. 'Come on,' he said quietly. 'I'll tell you about Gio.'

He had to help her to walk. Everything seemed to have shut down in her body: speech, thought, emotion, the will to move. Outside, the sympathetic-looking chauffeur was waiting, holding the door open for them. Did he know the secret? she wondered inconsequentially.

Luciano ordered his driver to find somewhere to park by the river and then asked him to disappear for an hour. They stayed in the car, sitting on the opposite side of the Thames to his office. Same view, different perspective—very different now. The whole world was different. She'd expected to be a divorcee soon. Instead, she was . . . a widow.

'You're cold.' He pulled a soft blanket from a box in front of them and wrapped it around her, his movements sympathetic and caring as she noticed for the first time that she'd been shivering uncontrollably.

She didn't want his tender concern. Irritably she pushed his hand away, miserably meeting his melting eyes when their fingers touched again. It would comfort her if she could lie in his arms and let the news sink in gradually. An overwhelming desire to be protected by him made her sit up stiffly as if he'd insulted her by presuming to show tenderness towards her.

'Don't touch me,' she grated, scared of her desire to be swept into Luciano's arms. 'Don't ever, ever touch me again!'

Immediately his manner became remote and polite as he opened up a drinks cabinet on the back of the driver's seat. 'I'm sorry, I thought you needed to be touched. Brandy or whisky?' he asked expressionlessly.

Both, she wanted to say. Oblivion would be fine. But she shrugged, unable to speak, and he poured her a brandy which she downed in one go.

Then she leaned her head back on the pillowy leather, smelling the richness of the interior, noticing details like the walnut trim and the deep pile of the carpet. She could hear Luciano's harsh but measured breathing, the sound when he swallowed, the ticking of his watch, and wondered hysterically why she was so acutely aware of everything at this moment when Gio must be aware of nothing.

'I feel so ashamed,' she mumbled.

'Why?' snapped Luciano warily.

And she flinched in alarm before her dense brain realised that he must be terribly on edge. 'I can't cry.'

Luciano relaxed, the taut line of his mouth easing a little, the distant manner softening. 'I said you would and you will,' he said gruffly. 'Shock is a means of protection for the mind, to allow a tragedy to be absorbed and dealt with. Don't be ashamed, Debbie; you have no reason for that. It's much better that you don't repress anything—but also that you don't force yourself to behave as convention dictates. Say whatever you want to say. Feel what you want to feel and think whatever you want to think.'

'Thank you,' she whispered appreciatively. 'Thank you for understanding.' It was a relief to know that he wouldn't condemn her because she wasn't sobbing her heart out. He had great strength and great sensitivity, she mused. A man of deep feelings and much experience. Gio's brother. How extraordinary...

'We all react differently.'

She lifted her dove-soft eyes to him and then hastily looked away. He seemed to be searching for words and she wasn't sure she wanted to know whatever he was going to tell her.

Silence settled between them, and her mind drifted. Luciano had surprised her with his understanding. It seemed that her emotions were whirling around in limbo. She felt sad, she felt sorrow. But there was anger and resentment and bitterness too. By refusing to talk about their relationship, by threatening to take Steffy away if they ever separated, Gio had robbed her of part of her life. And perhaps a chance of real happiness, with someone kind and caring.

Her huge eyes lifted to Luciano and she winced at the tenderness she saw in his expression.

'Are you all right?' he asked quietly.

'I'm sorry,' she said, blushing awkwardly. And she realised she'd been staring. 'I was... remembering.'

'Don't apologise,' he said, his eyes unreadable. 'Remember whatever gives you comfort. You have to be yourself.'

Colour stained her cheeks. But she *had* been unnerved by the way her vulnerable heart kept lurching in Luciano's direction.

'I don't want to remember,' she said mutinously.

He touched her fiery face with a questioning hand. 'Not of... moments with Gio?' he asked softly.

The purr of his voice made her tremble as it vibrated through her body. 'No, never again.' Her words turned into a horrid croak because she felt guilty that she wanted to put her awful marriage behind her, all the times that Gio had ridiculed her and made her cry.

Luciano nodded in understanding and her gaze meshed with his, sharing the raw pain that showed so clearly in his fathom-deep black eyes. 'It's all I've been doing all day,' he said quietly. 'Remembering.'

'I feel empty,' she admitted huskily, 'as if no one's at home.' Their eyes held. The tenderness of his gaze couldn't mask how weary he was. 'You're exhausted,' she said softly.

And certainly he no longer exuded that vital energy which had been so magnetic before. Now he seemed desperately in need of comfort himself. But she clenched her fists, stopping herself from touching his face in a sisterly caress and deliberately stopping herself from examining why she was so afraid of the slightest contact.

'I've had a lot to do.' He swirled the whisky around in his glass. 'I'm trying to make the arrangements from a distance.'

'It must have been such a shock,' she mumbled sympathetically. 'Especially as it came close on your discovery that Gio had a wife and not a casual girlfriend.' She shot him a nervous glance. 'Have you told your family yet?'

Luciano fiddled with the crease over his knee. 'No,' he admitted, finishing his drink.

She'd thought not. He'd have a difficult time, explaining that his brother had left a widow behind. She was about to mention Stefano when she thought better of it, deferring it till Luciano had told her why he'd brought her here to talk. It might be about something that would affect Steffy, and she must protect her son, even if it meant denying him the knowledge that his father had a family in Sicily.

'I'll go to the travel agent in the morning,' she said shakily, trying to hold on to mundane things.

'No.' Luciano took her hand in his firm grasp and fixed her with an intense stare that held her an instant prisoner. 'I think that would be very unwise. You must *not*,' he said fiercely. 'I beg you, for your own sake, change your mind. Forget the convention that you must say goodbye. Remember Gio as he was the last time you saw him and hold that in your heart. Don't let your last memory be unpleasant——'

'Please!' she gasped in distress, bewildered at his hard, biting tone.

'I have to be cruel to be kind,' he grated, gripping her hand so tightly that she almost welcomed the sense of pain because it meant she was alive after all. 'Tell me you won't go. Promise me,' he demanded grimly. 'You'd waste time and money by doing so.'

Her startled eyes widened, the lashes flickering frantically. 'What are time and money to me,' she asked hoarsely, 'when common decency tells me that I need to see my husband laid to rest? I have to be there, Luciano. I need . . . I need that ceremony to help me accept that he's gone. And you can't stop me. He was my husband.'

A devastating anguish swept across Luciano's face and she didn't cry out or protest against the unbearable crushing of her hand because she knew that he was unaware of it, and that he was struggling to find the words to tell her something he'd tried to keep from her.

'Not . . . exactly,' he rasped.

That was all he said. For a moment she didn't understand and continued with her gaze locked on his, trying to fathom out what he meant. What had she last said? 'He was my husband.' He'd replied, 'Not exactly.'

She dropped the glass, spilling brandy on her legs. But she hardly noticed. Life had returned fully to her body—a horrible, painful trembling that had Luciano releasing her hand and gently holding her arms while she shook like a woman with palsy.

The piece of the jigsaw. Pia. Gio's wife. It wasn't true. Please let it not be true.

Wanting to scream and wail, refusing to look into the darkness beyond his words, she tried to breathe more normally and hold herself together.

'How—how could he not exactly have been my husband?' she whispered through bone-dry lips.

Luciano took a while to answer. Then he took a deep breath and said, 'I'm sorry. I did everything I could to stop you finding this out. If you'd accepted my judgement and decided to stay in England instead of insisting on going to Sicily, you'd be none the wiser. But...'

'But what?' she whispered.

'He had a wife,' he said quietly.

Her heart missed a beat. 'Yes! Me!' she croaked, afraid to the very core of her being of what he was going to say.

'Another wife, not you. The one I told you about. Pia. I said she was my brother's wife. Do you remember?' he said gently. 'Pia is the one who has the franchise for City Lights...'

She moaned. Once, deep from the core of her being. 'No!' she cried, fighting him, fighting the hateful thing he'd said with all her might. He was lying. Gio wouldn't do that to her... Oh, dear God, he wouldn't. 'No, no, *no*!' she rasped.

'Hit me,' he growled. 'Go on, hit me if you must.'

'How dare you?' she screamed hysterically, doing just that. 'You brute! You foul-mouthed, lying brute! I *was* married to Gio—we had a wedding!' she yelled, punctuating her words with hard, hurting punches that had Luciano grunting as each blow landed. 'Mother wore a pink hat and I had a blue suit and my best friend...'

She paused, briefly shocked into silence. Tracy had begged her not to marry Gio and said he wasn't to be trusted. Refusing to acknowledge her doubts, she resumed her furious onslaught on the undefended Luciano. 'My best friend had her hair cut!' she cried wildly, as if that would make everything real for him. 'I have the certificate. I can show it to you...'

She didn't know how long she went on shouting at Luciano and hitting him—only that suddenly she began to sob with a dreadful violence that she'd never experienced before in the whole of her life. And Luciano had taken her in his arms and was holding her safe and secure while she cried till she could only heave up great dry, racking sobs from her hollow stomach.

'I can't bear it,' she sobbed over and over again. 'I can't bear it, I c-c-can't.'

And then she lay as still as death, pale, limp and helpless, her lips pouting unhappily, her wet lashes blinking back the tears.

He was stroking her hair, his mouth warm on her scalp. She lay supine, exhausted, with her head nuzzled against the soft black cloth of his jacket, hardly breathing at all. Luciano had relaxed back into the seat and she stared miserably at his gently rising chest, overwhelmed by a feeling of bitterness that she had been betrayed so thoroughly.

'Another woman,' she croaked, understanding everything at last. 'Another *wife*!'

He stirred and she realised that she'd spoken out loud. Gently he turned her chin up and for a terrible moment she held her breath in alarm because she thought that he might kiss her. Then he frowned at her mouth and she compressed the lips she had unknowingly allowed to flower. Oh, God, she thought, shocked by her reaction, and put it down to emotion, to her loss, her terrible need for comfort and reassurance and love.

'Now you see why you can't go, don't you?' he said gravely.

'No. I'm the one who was Gio's wife,' she said stubbornly. 'Pia was...' Her heart lurched with a sudden thought. 'I *was* the legal wife, wasn't I?' Her words hung in the air and she watched the raw anguish fill Luciano's eyes with mounting horror.

'No. You weren't.'

Her eyes closed in brief agony. So matter-of-fact. Her whole life in turmoil, the brief years of her marriage a farce, a lie, and Luciano was slicing her heart in two with cold fact.

When she raised her eyes plaintively to him again, she saw that his expression was stern and unyielding. 'You can't go, Debbie,' he said quietly. 'Pia will be there. You can't——'

'Rock the boat,' she muttered bitterly. 'No one will want to meet Gio's bit on the side!'

'Don't put yourself down; he must have loved you.' Luciano gave her a wintry smile, his breath filtering sweetly over her face. 'He'd find it hard not to,' he added huskily.

She didn't know what to make of that. Perhaps it had been to console her, because it wasn't true. Gio had lied to her and had cheated Stefano of legitimacy. Steffy! What would she tell him?

'Oh, God,' she moaned, letting Luciano's fingers soothe the beating pulses at her temples. 'When—when did he marry Pia?'

'A long time ago. When he was eighteen.'

Gio had recently had his twenty-ninth birthday. She winced. He'd said he wouldn't be able to celebrate his birthday at home. Perhaps he had gone to his other home, in Sicily. Her mouth grew bitter.

'We married four years ago; I was twenty-one,' she mumbled, refusing to torment herself with too many questions.

'I didn't want to tell you. As I said before, I suspected he had someone else he was visiting regularly because he kept disappearing,' Luciano said grimly. 'But I didn't know the truth till you appeared in my office—and even then I was reluctant to accept what my brother had done.'

Her mind whirled. '*Why*?' she jerked out. 'Why would he do this to me? Because I wouldn't sleep with him when we first met?'

'Perhaps. I imagine he found you very alluring.' Luciano's velvety tones vibrated through her body. 'He's always had whatever he's wanted. I don't want to talk about him,' he growled. 'Debbie, close the door on your time with Gio. Remember everything that was good and carry on with your life. I still don't want you to go to the funeral.'

'Because of the scandal?' she asked resentfully.

'Because you'll be hurt. You won't be at all welcome. Think how uncomfortable you'd feel,' he said persuasively. 'There will be hostility towards you if you turn up; we're a close-knit family. I doubt that you could handle the venom that would be directed towards you. And you'd hurt Pia, of course.'

'I don't want to do that,' she said in a low voice. No matter what Pia Colleoni had done to wreck her business... Debbie tensed. 'I think Pia might have known about me!' she exclaimed huskily. 'Do you think that's why she directed all her energy towards ruining Mum and me?'

'Perhaps. I don't know. Jealousy...jealousy does odd things to people. You covet what someone else has...'

Speculatively, Luciano's fingers drifted down her throat, rendering Debbie speechless. Wide-eyed, she swallowed and flushed when she saw his expression harden, as if he'd seen her reaction and found it offensive under the circumstances. She couldn't help it. Heaven help her, something was hurling her feelings around without caring where they landed.

'Please don't do that,' she whispered.

'I wasn't thinking. Forgive me. You've had a bad time,' he said gravely. 'You need your mother. I'll take you home now.'

The caress was withdrawn. Debbie gave a sigh of regret before she realised that she'd done so and hastily lowered her lashes to hide her disappointment. Comfort. She was hungry for comfort. That was what it had been all along—a need for a man to hold her in his arms and make her feel special.

Gio had only ever held her when he wanted sex, not when she'd wanted cuddles or consoling after a tough day. He hadn't consoled her when her hair went frizzy in the rain and stuck out everywhere and made him laugh and tease her about looking like a haystack. Nor whenever she worried about her mother's health and wanted a strong shoulder to worry on.

Now Luciano was showing all the signs of being a man who had deep feelings, who would look further than her outer shell and offer the comfort she needed. And she was so distressed by everything that had happened that her mind was confusing her gratitude for his kind protection with something more significant.

'Yes,' she mumbled, realising she had to escape to safety before she made a fool of herself. 'I need my mother. I need to think—to come to terms with what's happened.'

Her marriage was finally, officially over—in fact it had never really existed. She had to mourn that and then sweep the lies under the table and forget them. For Stefano's sake. He was all she had left.

Luciano nodded, his dark eyes gentle. 'We may not meet again. But... I want to say that I would have liked to have known you under different circumstances,' he said softly.

Meeting his molten black eyes, she felt a quiver run through the whole length of her body. And fought it. 'He and I—we did love one another,' she said shakily, wanting to convince Luciano that she hadn't married for some shallow whim or youthful stupidity. They had loved one another, some time in the past. She must have done, but she couldn't remember when or how it had felt. And that made her eyes fill with tears.

'Of course you did.' He drew far away from her, into the corner of the car, his face dark and shuttered. 'Everyone loved Gio.'

There had been something savage in his tone, as though he considered that Gio had never been worthy of such unquestioning love. But she didn't want to ask him to elaborate. For Steffy's sake she must hold in her heart the few things that had been good.

'Take me home,' she said unsteadily. 'I want my mother.'

'Certainly.'

He was the clipped, efficient businessman again. Slipping out of the car for a moment, he searched the street for his driver and caught the man's eye, speaking quietly to him for a moment or two. Debbie was surprised when the chauffeur caught Luciano's arms in sympathetic friendship while he listened.

They left the silky black Thames and the romantic outline of Tower Bridge. Across the water was the Tower itself, the ghostly grey walls a monument to centuries of triumphs and disappointments, mystery and intrigue. Both she and Luciano stared at the Tower till it had gone from view, its bleak walls mirroring her feelings.

Her tears began to fall silently. Luciano looked across at her. She felt him hesitate for a moment and then deliberately turn his back on her. The shock of his rejection made her weep helplessly for a reason she couldn't fathom.

'We're here.' He sounded curt, detached.

Emotion robbed her of speech. Without a word, she stumbled out. Slammed the door. Walked to the shop without a goodbye, without acknowledging Luciano at all. She had decisions to make. The hardest decision of all being whether to go to Sicily or stay home. To rock the boat, or to stay safely in harbour.

If she did go to the funeral, she and Luciano would become enemies because he'd made it clear that he didn't want her to go. And she'd have to face the contempt of his family. Yet if she didn't pay her last respects to the man who'd fathered her son she would never lay Gio to rest in her heart.

And she couldn't even ask her mother for guidance because she wasn't going to tell her about Gio's deception. His death would be enough of a shock for her to cope with.

Trembling, she opened the door as the Bentley glided away and Luciano Colleoni left her life. Her eyes closed in anguish and she collapsed in a pitiful heap at the bottom of the stairs, her heart breaking with an unidentifiable pain.

She was alone. Terribly alone. And she'd been so hurt that she knew she would turn in on herself and remain alone for a very long time.

Her heart and her mind turned to Gio at last and her shattered illusions became muddled in the outpouring of her silent tears. Whether she cried for Gio or herself, or for his betrayal of her trust, she didn't know. But she wept till her body was empty and then she went up to tell her mother.

CHAPTER FOUR

TEN days had passed. Ten days and Luciano had telephoned her from Sicily on every one of those days. On the day before she set off for Sicily herself, she felt very much on edge waiting for his call, nervous of travelling, uncomfortable because she felt guilty at deceiving Luciano.

'Debbie. Hello.' His warm tones floated into her ear, setting her pulses racing, and she sank into a chair, curling up to enjoy the chat.

'Hello, Luciano,' she said, feeling like a shy teenager talking to her first boyfriend. Her hands were so *shaky*. She tried to sound less breathy. 'Thanks for putting that business our way. I'm really grateful.'

'No problem. Anything else I can do for you? I have some spare cash—an "excess of liquidity", my accountant calls it,' he said, and she imagined he must be smiling, 'and I could invest it in equipment for you or——'

'No, thanks. You're being very kind,' she answered gratefully, 'but we're managing very well now that the competition is fair again. Mum says thank you for speaking to the people at City Lights. We've taken on two more staff and we're at our limit now.'

'I didn't want to offend you,' he explained. 'But I don't want you to go short. I want to help.'

'You have,' she assured him. 'You have.'

'And . . . you're all right?' he asked delicately.

'Yes, I am. Honestly.' She hesitated. This could be the last time they spoke together and she wanted to tell him about Steffy but decided it might be better not to. There would be complications if he knew that his brother had a child and she couldn't cope with that at the moment. 'Work helps. Things are looking up. I can make a good life for Mother and me now, I'm sure.'

'I'm so glad. You deserve some good luck. If there's ever anything I can do, just give me a call. Advice, a friendly ear, experts you need to find like asset managers.' The rich warmth in his tone made her smile happily. He was genuinely delighted for her. But she was deceiving him...

'More likely plumbers and decorators,' she said wryly.

He laughed. 'Oh, those too. Seriously. I have my own; they'd be a lot cheaper than anyone else. Let me help you, Debbie,' he added huskily. 'I'd like to help. I like to think of you working in that kitchen with your mother, cooking, singing, talking.'

There was a silence. Debbie felt a little choked up. 'Luciano,' she said hesitantly, 'whatever happens, you won't feel badly about me, will you?'

'Never,' he answered emphatically. 'Unless... you're not thinking of travelling to Sicily, are you?' he asked, suddenly stern.

'You've told me not to,' she said evasively, her heart thudding at the deliberate avoidance of the truth.

'I care about you. I don't want you to be hurt.'

She swallowed at the intense concern in his voice. He cared. And that touched her heart, making her happy and nervous at the same time. 'I—I won't be,' she mumbled, and invented a crisis because she knew she'd break down and confess her plans if he was any kinder. 'The cakes! Must go!' she cried in a genuine panic.

'Then go. Ring me later. Bye.'

The receiver stayed in her hand because it was a link with him and she didn't want to break that link. 'Oh, Luciano,' she said in dismay.

He'd been so caring and she was letting him down. Perhaps, she mused sadly, there was something else more important that she was putting in jeopardy—a warmth between them that had promised a deeper friendship. He made her feel protected and caressed with his caring and that was something she'd prefer not to lose.

Debbie sighed. When she got back, she'd have to confess what she'd done—since her plan meant that he'd never even know she'd attended Gio's funeral—and maybe they could become real friends.

Palermo terrified her, as Luciano had predicted. She'd never ventured beyond the boundaries of Greater London before. The drive from the Punta Raisi airport had her clutching her seat in fear of her life as the taxi wove in and out of the ill-disciplined and erratically be-haved traffic. People seemed to have scant regard for their safety, stepping into the road whenever the fancy took them, and she was relieved when she was deposited at the *economico* hotel which the taxi driver had suggested.

It was then, watching Stefano sleeping soundly in the loneliness of the tiny, basic room, that the enormity of her actions swept over her. Since telling her mother of Gio's death, and sitting in frozen numbness while her mother held her cold, emotionless body, she hadn't cried. All she'd felt was a sadness because she and Gio had wasted part of their lives in a dead relationship.

Spilt milk. It was over now, though first she must check on where the funeral was to be held. Taking the map with her, she ran down the narrow stairs to the small bar, where the English-speaking manager sat nursing a beer.

'Can you point out the Villa di Leoni on this map?' she asked politely. And she blessed City Lights for once; she knew where to go because she'd telephoned her rivals and pretended to be a favoured customer, enquiring after Pia Colleoni.

'Leoni . . . *Al funerale*?' he suggested and she nodded. 'Gio Colleoni . . . *Amica*? Friend?' Surprised, but imagining that the crash must have been in the newspaper, she nodded again and the man lifted a grizzled eyebrow. '*Molte amiche*,' he said cynically. 'Many friends.'

Female friends? Sick to the stomach at the thought, she grimly quelled the awful ideas flying around her head by scuttling back up the stairs and making plans. Tomorrow she'd collect the hire car she'd ordered in England, buy some food and things that Stefano needed, and drive east. The journey would be quite straightforward—if she ever got out of Palermo alive.

And then she'd position herself where she could see the funeral but not be seen. She had decided that that was the best solution. A compromise. Her farewell would be private and she wouldn't hurt anyone's feelings.

Carefully, wanting to keep her borrowed and slightly ill-fitting black suit tidy, she removed it and hung it on the wire hanger in the rickety wardrobe.

Debbie gazed wistfully at the telephone. It would be lovely to ring her mother, but she didn't dare spend any more of her borrowed money than was necessary. Things were going to be very tight from now on. The future was something she didn't want to face yet.

Deciding to save on expenses by going without supper, she slipped into the narrow bed beside Steffy. She was incapable of pushing any food down her anyway, and had worried her family by being sick every time she did.

Her mother, aunts, uncles and cousins had all offered to come with her and their kindness had made her cry. None of them had offered to make the journey because they wanted to pay their respects to Gio. Her family hadn't liked him, she knew that. They'd tried to like him for her sake.

Of course, she had had to refuse their offers to accompany her, since they'd discover that she wasn't an official mourner. Her family would find out that she'd never been legally married at all and that Gio had been a bigamist. That was a secret she must keep forever. She felt her stomach tighten with tension and clutched the pillow, gritting her teeth against the recurring nausea.

Her head burrowed into the pillow and she stroked Steffy's downy cheek, feeling immediately calmer. Being with him would be enough to comfort her. And when he was grown-up she'd tell him he had said goodbye to his daddy and he'd be glad.

The next day, Wednesday, was hot, though a cool breeze swept down from the mass of green-clad mountains which backed the small village of Castelleoni. Nervous and edgy, she parked the car in the small cobbled road that led to the pretty Byzantine church and lifted Stefano from the car seat.

'Remember this, sweetheart,' she whispered fiercely into his neat little ear, and popped on his sailor sunhat. 'Look at the blue sky, Steffy. Look at the birds.' She pointed to the swallows, wheeling and piping that wonderful sound of summer promise. 'Isn't it lovely and warm?'

'Tree,' he cried cheerfully, waving his arm at the avenue of shady plane trees that led to the church.

'Lots of trees,' she said fondly, and tucked him on her hip, smiling faintly when he waggled the brim of her black felt hat.

He'd help her to get over this. Help her, too, to cope with the coming moments when she'd see Pia and the Colleoni family. Maybe Luciano. Her heart gave an extra tremor of nervous anticipation. Luciano would be there and he'd never know she was watching him.

Hollow-eyed, she stared at the tiny whitewashed church with its gilt dome, the field beside it packed with limousines, confirming that the mourners were inside.

The bells were tolling. Out here in the fresh, country air, the banks tumbling with wild flowers and sheep's bells tinkling in the distance, the heavy, funereal sound seemed unduly sombre and out of place. Villagers were standing around talking, many of them, despite the sunshine, wearing coats. People who must have known Gio as a boy and watched him grow up with his family. Debbie's eyes glittered with anger.

'Come to the garden,' she said, putting Stefano down and taking his hand. She led him to the graveyard, stopping so that he could pick purple clover, late buttercups and blue vetch which he held in his small fist in delight. There they waited.

Mingling with the respectful villagers, she watched sadly as the coffin was brought out. She looked around for Stefano, but he'd been claimed by a group of cooing women who had devoted themselves to his amusement, and she didn't like to draw attention to herself by slipping through the gathering to collect him. He was safe and happy. It was enough that he was there with her.

Her eyes took in the rather sinister-looking black-clad family, searching first for Luciano. Her hopes lifted in anticipation and then fell like a stone. He wasn't there. Disappointment hit her like a physical blow.

And then a heavy hand clamped on her shoulder, a hand that shot life through her body, and Luciano's fierce whisper came.

'What the hell are you doing here? You fool! You stupid fool!'

She whirled in alarm and there he was, dark and scowling and creating a storm of emotion within her. 'I have a right,' she declared shakily, tilting up her head proudly till the brim of her hat touched the back of her neck. 'I'm not intruding. Let me be, Luciano,' she pleaded when his mouth tightened menacingly. 'I needed to come.'

He flinched. Angry with his reaction and upset that she seemed unable to bear the fact that he wasn't glad to see her, she hastily turned around to watch the ceremony.

'You're taking one hell of a risk,' he muttered.

'I—I had to come. Can't you see that? No one will know who I am,' she said jerkily.

'I do hope you're going away immediately this is finished?' he growled, far too close to her shoulder.

She would go and that would be the end of her link with him because he was obviously furious at being disobeyed. Very macho—and she'd thought better of him. He didn't care about her needs at all. Despair welled up in her heart and she wasn't sure why. For Gio? Herself? For something she'd hoped for in vain?

'Yes,' she said. Tension quivered in the air between them. She resented his anger with her and her stomach was lurching around because he was so close. She could hear and feel his breathing, sense him with the whole of her body.

And she felt guilty, too, that his compelling presence was drawing her whole-hearted attention away from Gio. 'Go away,' she whispered fiercely, flashing her furious eyes up at him. 'How can you intrude at a time like this?'

There was a tightening of the skin across his cheekbones as he glared back at her. 'Keep a hold of yourself,' he muttered. 'People will wonder why you're so upset. God, you must be mad to have made the journey! It was stupid in the extreme. You don't know what you're risking. If you cause any trouble——'

'Do you honestly think I would?' she cut in rawly, the hurt showing in her limpid grey eyes.

'I've no idea. Just don't cry and don't let yourself be seen,' he muttered harshly. 'Try to merge into the background.'

He was afraid, she told herself miserably. Scared that she'd feel compelled to announce her presence and cause a scandal in front of everyone. 'I don't *want* to be seen,' she seethed. 'Go away. Go back to the family where you belong.'

'I can't. I've been banned,' he answered savagely.

Astonished, she watched him walk away, a proud and lonely figure, striding angrily through the deferential path created by the villagers. He didn't stop. Debbie held her breath, seeing where he was heading and dreading what would come next. He didn't stop till he came to the women grouped around the fair-haired Stefano, who'd been wrapped in a black shawl against the supposedly chill air and was munching on a small cake.

Luciano greeted and spoke to the women, caressing Steffy's little pink cheek. The look on his face made her heart lurch. He didn't know this was his brother's child, she thought, her eyes filling with the poignancy of the moment.

Steffy was chortling, grabbing Luciano's hand, refusing to let go. With enormous difficulty, Debbie turned back to watch the ceremony, her emotions shredded by the sight of Luciano and her son. Silent tears streamed down her cheeks as the coffin was lowered and she didn't know whether Luciano witnessed that moment or not.

Her whole body screamed to be allowed to turn and check on him. Her mind overruled that urge but the scene ahead became blurred and she was only conscious that several pretty women near by were crying. Earlier she'd taken a quick glance at them, noted their blonde hair, their voluptuous figures and had coped with the lacerating pain that had filled her heart. These could be the 'friends' spoken of so knowingly by the hotel manager.

Her hands trembled. Was Gio's reputation so bad that it was common knowledge?

The smell of lemony herbs mingled with orange blossom in the grove beyond the whitewashed church. The magnificent cone of the snow-capped Mount Etna reared up in the background, a thin plume of smoke drifting from the crater. And the villagers, all in black, murmured respectfully waiting for the family to disperse.

Suddenly a cry rang out—Steffy's imperious, piercing little voice. 'Mum-mum!'

Startled, she turned, knuckling the tears of lost hopes away. To her horror, she saw a stony-faced Luciano holding Steffy, who was waving at her with that sweet opening and closing of his hand that never failed to pull at her heart-strings.

And Steffy continued to shout, 'Mum-mum!' gleefully at her.

Both she and Luciano were rooted to the spot. She had no idea what her face told him, knew only that he had gone as white as a sheet.

Her heart sank. 'Oh, no,' she groaned helplessly, seeing the fury lighting his eyes. 'No,' she whispered, cursing fate for its bad timing.

Briefly, Luciano looked down at Steffy's joyful face. Presumably looking for confirmation that this was her child, he gently folded back the peasant shawl. He revealed the red jumper she'd knitted for Steffy and the red jogging pants covered in Mickey Mouse patterns that even she knew were very un-Sicilian. No chance of pretending he belonged to someone else, then. She'd have to hear him call her son a bastard, suffer his questions, listen to his demands that she make no attempt to blackmail the family.

As if she would. Her dearest wish was to get home and throw herself into work. To forget the magnetic Luciano who made her restless and underlined her sense of emptiness every time she put the phone down after his calls. To forget the pain and the misery and the shame that she'd never be able to live down and could never share with another living soul.

Deceit and secrets were alien to her. Already she'd told more lies to her family about the arrangements for the funeral than she'd ever dreamed of. There would be more to come when she got back and they asked how things had gone.

Please, her eyes said to Luciano. Please don't make an issue of this.

He came towards her, looking grim, while Steffy settled happily in his arms and did his little wave, his expression more and more puzzled when she didn't respond. So she lifted a heavy hand and half-heartedly did their special open-close wave.

'Hello, sweetheart,' she said shakily, reaching for Stefano when Luciano came close enough. 'Have you had a lovely time?'

'Yes. Nice lady. Nice cake,' he said enthusiastically, flinging his arms around her neck. 'More cake?' he enquired hopefully.

'No more. Look at you,' she said fondly, rustling up a faint smile. 'There's chocolate all round your mouth.'

Steffy lifted his face and squeezed his eyes tightly, waiting for the inevitable cleaning-up operation. He was adorable, she thought with a sentimental pang. The joy of her life.

Somehow ignoring Luciano, she fumbled for the clasp on her bag and a tissue-wipe but he got there before she did, solemnly using a soft linen handkerchief to brush away the crumbs and gently remove the smears of chocolate that artificially widened Stefano's rosebud mouth.

Debbie trembled, intimidated by Luciano's closeness, by the intimacy and tenderness of his action. 'Thank you,' she said politely. And huskily. Blushing, she fought for normality.

Luciano replaced his handkerchief and the dark eyes blazed beneath the lowered black brows. 'This is your son?' he hurled at her.

'Mine and Gio's,' she said in quiet defiance.

He followed the recent trail of her tears down her cheeks, his expression inscrutable. But he swore savagely under his breath and the tension in his body made her nervous. 'You didn't say you had a child,' he said heavily.

'You never asked.'

'Mummy cry,' said Stefano anxiously as a new tear welled from her eye.

She managed to give him a wavering smile. 'Mummy's laughing now,' she said reassuringly, baring her teeth and hoping that would do. Deftly, she twisted the black rose off her hat since Steffy seemed bent on demolishing it otherwise, and was relieved when he became engrossed in the way the petals curled around his fat finger. 'Don't upset him,' she mouthed to Luciano.

'You should have told me.'

She shot him a resentful look. 'Why? I have a son. What difference does it make to you?' she snapped and suddenly strode away.

She couldn't stand being near him, seeing his icy contempt, his anger that she'd disobeyed his autocratic orders and had actually dared to attend the funeral of the man she'd believed to be her husband.

'It makes a lot of difference—all the difference in the world.' He'd kept up with her and caught her elbow. A shot of pure adrenalin rushed through her arm, making her gasp. Dismayed, she turned it into a growl of irritation.

'Get out of my way,' she spat, pressing Steffy close to her body defensively. 'I want to visit the grave when

the family's gone—and I don't want you around. I need
to be alone. Can't you see that? Luciano! Don't you
have any pity for me at all?' she cried jerkily. 'I lived
with your brother as his wife...' Her voice faltered at
the deeply bitter expression on his face. 'Leave me alone.
I want to be alone.'

'Gio,' he muttered harshly. 'Gio, Gio, Gio.' His grip
tightened briefly and then fell away. 'You did love him,
then. I wondered...' His mouth thinned. 'Go and say
goodbye to the man you loved, then. Tell your son...'

His liquid gaze dropped to study the absorbed Steffy,
and Debbie trembled uncontrollably at the gentle softness
of Luciano's parted lips as his eyes lingered on her son's
pale blond hair and the impossibly long black lashes that
concealed the deep brown eyes he'd inherited from Gio.

'He is so innocent...' Luciano sighed. 'Tell your son
how much his father was adored by everyone,' he continued huskily. 'Give him all the memories, all the stories
you wish.' His head lifted and she was lanced by two
merciless eyes. 'But if you value the love you have between you and your mother, the life you have in England
with your friends and close family, then leave here and
never come back, never try to contact me or anyone in
my family. Because, by God,' he growled, 'your life will
be ripped apart if you do.'

'You're afraid I'll cause trouble. I wouldn't dream of
it; I might be poor but I have my pride,' she said stiffly.
'I wouldn't want to be involved with your family. I *want*
to go home. I want my own family around me. I love
them and they love me, and,' she said, anger and distress and despair irrationally making her want to hurt
him, 'that's more than your family does, isn't it? I don't
envy you and your wealth. I pity you because your family
has banished you from the burial of your brother. Envy
me, Luciano!' she cried fervently, her heart unac-
countably near to breaking because she was his enemy

now. 'I have love and I have Steffy who is more precious to me than anything in this world. *Envy* me.'

'You're blind,' he growled. 'Blind to what's in front of your face. I suppose,' he added bitterly, 'I must thank God you are.'

Seething with suppressed emotion, he spun on his heel and marched towards the grave which the family had just left, every inch of his body quivering as if he wanted to erupt with the passions within him. He stood for a moment, perhaps offering a silent prayer, and Debbie waited till she could go there too, trembling from head to foot from the bitter encounter.

He was terribly upset at losing his brother, of course. But there was something more, some undefinable fury that racked him and tore into his heart. She knew it, sensed it with the antennae she seemed to possess whenever he was near. And she hadn't understood what he'd said. He seemed to think she was missing some significant fact, and he was glad.

'Look, cat! Down! Down!' Steffy squealed with delight, wriggling in her arms and thrusting the rose back at her. 'Please,' he remembered beguilingly.

Debbie managed a wavering smile. Steffy had defused the situation again. 'All right, darling. Be kind to the cat. Stroke it very gently, the way I showed you,' she reminded him, setting him on the grass.

When she straightened, she saw that the family was walking past, and she found herself eye to eye with an elegant and petite blonde. The woman narrowed her eyes when Debbie blushed and then mercifully walked on. Debbie let out her breath, knowing it must be... She forced herself to think the awful words. It must be Gio's widow.

Curiosity made her stare at the woman's back. Pia was dainty and beautifully groomed, with corn-coloured hair that had, like Debbie's, been sternly swept into a neat chignon beneath her hat. It seemed almost a betrayal that Pia should be blonde like her, and should be small and neat—the kind of woman men liked to protect. Debbie had always longed to be tiny, instead of towering over half the men in London.

A groan escaped her pale lips as the reality of her situation hammered itself home. Pia was beautiful, not a monster. He'd probably enjoyed being with such a well-groomed and clearly well-bred woman.

Whereas she… Debbie grimaced. She was the woman Gio had 'married' because that was the only way he could get her into bed, but he'd only used her as a pastime while his real wife was busy. A diversion. Damn him, she thought, clenching her jaw tightly in anger.

How long, she wondered, before she stopped feeling dirty? Before she lost the now all too familiar wash of horror and sickness that came whenever she thought of her farce of a marriage?

Debbie's unhappy eyes had followed Pia. The woman paused by the entrance to the field where the cars were parked and her back stiffened as if she felt Debbie's scrutiny. Wanting to move and hide, Debbie felt compelled to watch in mounting apprehension as Pia turned and the two women's eyes clashed like swords.

And Debbie knew that she suspected. How, she didn't know, but guilt made her flush with mortification when Pia's dark brown eyes widened in recognition.

'It is you! You are the bitch!' Pia screamed suddenly in perfect English, her voice carrying past the startled villagers. 'You *slut*.'

'No,' whispered Debbie, appalled by the sea of faces staring at her.

'So, you come to Sicily,' shrieked Pia, advancing unsteadily over the grass on her spindly heels. 'You insult me by showing your common little face in a cheap, chain-store suit that only a trollop like you would wear——'

'*Pia.*'

Everyone jumped at Luciano's roar, which came from some distance away, and Debbie wanted to sink to the ground in shame. So she looked like a slut. She looked cheap.

She flung a frantic glance at Steffy, who was happily curled up with the huge black cat, ignoring everything around him. Her heart leapt in relief. If only she could be as innocent as her son. Oblivious, blameless... But she wasn't. In the eyes of the law she had slept with another woman's husband and to all intents and purposes she was a tramp.

'I—I'm n-not what you say,' she stuttered miserably as Pia flounced to within a yard of her.

'You and all of them,' spat Pia, waving an arm that included her in the group of sniffing blondes. 'But you are the worst, the most evil,' she added, obviously consumed with hatred.

'No, I'm not,' protested Debbie in abject misery. Luciano was approaching fast. He looked angry enough to hit her. She groaned, aghast. Her plan hadn't worked out. She'd upset Pia and was embarrassing the family and she'd never forgive herself. Nor would he forgive the slur on the Colleoni name. 'It wasn't like that; I didn't know... I didn't mean to——'

'Seductress!' hissed Pia furiously.

'*No*! I'm sorry,' wailed Debbie. 'I'm sorry! I wish——'

'Shut up, Pia,' ordered Luciano roughly, grabbing his sister-in-law and giving her a shake.

A stream of words flowed from Pia's bitter lips, obviously dreadful insults because the villagers near by looked shocked. The women who'd cuddled Stefano were now muttering and hurling insults of their own at Debbie, bracketing her as a scarlet woman, no doubt, who'd lured Gio away from his lawful wife.

'I didn't know. I didn't know,' she sobbed.

She had to go. Half blinded by the tears, scarlet with shame, she stumbled over to Stefano, who was looking at her uncertainly, his lip beginning to quiver. Desperate to get away from the accusing eyes, she scooped up her son who immediately yelled in protest.

'No! Want cat! Mummy! Mummy!' he wailed in temper, pushing at her mouth angrily with his small hand.

'Fool!' Luciano growled savagely at her as she hurried past him.

'You *told* her about me, you swine,' she jerked, flashing him a look of pure hatred.

'How the hell could I?' he snarled. 'I haven't spoken to her.'

It didn't matter. She'd been identified and held up in front of everyone as a tramp. There was an undercurrent of murmurs all around her and she pressed the knuckles of one hand to her mouth as she marched along, stifling her scream of despair.

Steffy mustn't be involved in this any longer. He mustn't remember this horrible atmosphere of hatred and loathing. Appalled that Gio's funeral should have been so embarrassingly disrupted, she bent her head and hurried miserably through the contemptuous villagers.

'Steffy, please, please,' she begged plaintively, when he continued to demand his right to stroke the cat. But at least his complaints concentrated her mind and shut out those dark faces all around her, those malicious mouths. 'We'll find another cat,' she promised shakily. He struggled sulkily and he was so heavy now that she almost fell with his weight shift. So she did something she'd never done before—she resorted to bribery. 'Steffy,' she said desperately, 'I'll buy you a cat. Let's go home and buy one, shall we?'

He beamed and hugged her and she groaned in relief. They'd almost reached the top of the cobbled road where she'd left the car. This terrible day would be over soon, she thought shakily, resolutely setting her sights on the future.

'Down! Want walk!' demanded Stefano.

'No, sweetheart. When we get to the car——'

Debbie stiffened. She'd heard a sound that made her groan again, this time in dismay. Someone was running after her. Not Luciano. A woman's feet. Not Pia's, she thought breathlessly, increasing her pace. The sound suggested heavier shoes.

'*Dio mio*! *Prego mi aspetti*! Wait, please wait!' came a husky, despairing woman's cry.

She wasn't going to stay and be insulted. It hadn't been her fault. Oh, damn, she wailed silently in disappointment. How could this happen to me? And to Steffy? This had been the most awful day of her life and she wanted it to end, to turn her back on the Colleoni family and build her shattered life again.

Grimly she carried on running, her breathing heavy because of the struggling, complaining Steffy, who thought at this moment of all moments that being carried was babyish. The nightmare would end. It must. Soon. All she had to do was get to the car, strap Steffy in...

The key. She couldn't find the key. 'Oh, please, please,' she begged her guardian angel, almost sobbing with panic. Because now she could hear a man's long, loping run coming along the path—Luciano, or one of those dark, sinister men who'd been in the family party. 'Oh, help!' The door was open. 'Stef, don't be cross, darling,' she sniffed miserably, kissing his little nose when he stubbornly kicked in frustration. Poor darling, he didn't understand why she was being so curt with him. 'Please don't be cross; I can't stand it. We have to go——'

'You can't go now. Whether you or I like it or not, you have to face the music. We have no choice—it's a matter of honour. I wish... Hell, woman, you've stirred up a hornets' nest!' came Luciano's savage tones.

'Go away!' she yelled. 'Oh, Steffy, let me do the straps up,' she cried in agitation.

'No! Shan't!' he defied.

'I'll deal with your son,' Luciano growled.

'No,' she gasped, battling with toddler and car seat and tears. 'I'm going,' she yelled over Stefano's repeated 'shan't', 'and you're not touching him!'

'Be quiet, both of you!' Luciano roared, stunning Steffy into an astonished silence.

Debbie blinked and Steffy blinked back, his eyes solemn and subdued. No one had ever spoken sharply to him before, let alone shouted. Gio had insisted that Stefano should be indulged. 'He is my son; he will have whatever he wants,' he'd said grandly and Debbie had worked hard to merge her ideas on child-rearing with his as she believed that children needed love and kindness, but firmness too.

Two strong hands gripped her waist, rendering her helpless. The stuffing went out of her legs and she became horrifyingly limp and malleable. She wanted to surrender, to allow Luciano to whip her with his contempt and anger, because grief had weakened her and she had no fight left in her.

Helplessly she felt him draw her back. Then he pushed her against the car, such fury on his face that she flattened herself against the metal in terror.

'I said you'd regret it if you ever revealed yourself to the family,' he said menacingly. 'And, by God, you will.' He dipped his head into the back of the car as if to snatch Steffy from his seat. '*Why* do you have to be so stubborn? Why bring attention to yourself?'

'I didn't. And ... no! What are you doing? You're not to touch my child!' yelled Debbie in horror.

Her sense of protection towards Stefano was so great that she succeeded in dragging Luciano out again. Her hat had come off, her hair was spilling from its pins in an uncontrolled golden river and she flushed at his grim glance; he was comparing her with the immaculate Pia.

'Oh, curse you all,' she wailed. 'And leave Steffy alone,' she rasped hoarsely, her breasts heaving with panic. 'Touch a hair of his head and I swear I'll kill you!'

Luciano flinched. 'You insult me,' he said tightly, looking down on her from his haughty height. 'To suggest that I'd harm a child...!' His nostrils flared with fury.

'I—I'm sorry,' she muttered in contrition.

'Now I know what you think of me,' he said tightly. 'And that gives me a free rein to behave as I please without concerning myself with your sensibilities. Now get in the car!'

'I was going to,' she grated, but when she went to get into the driver's seat she found her arm had been caught in his strong grip. 'Oh, make up your wretched mind,' she cried, half hysterical with emotion.

'Get in the passenger seat,' he growled. 'I am driving.'

Her eyes widened. 'You? Why?' she gasped.

'Because,' snapped a female voice—the same husky voice that had called after her, begging her to wait, 'there are things to be talked about. Is that not so, Luciano?'

Luciano looked at the veiled woman coldly. 'Unfortunately there are, much as I dislike the prospect. Under the circumstances, you may go to the house,' he said to the woman in stilted tones. 'All of you.'

And, taking advantage of Debbie's astonishment, he pushed her into the car and slammed the door, daring her with a stern glare to open it again.

'Who was that?' she asked warily.

'My...' There was an odd little pause. 'My mother.'

She quailed, both at the cold, unloving tones and the fact that she'd put herself in such a bad light with Steffy's grandmother. Her mind whirled. She had a choice: to leap out, try to undo the buckles on Steffy's car seat and run somewhere with him—where?—through that hostile crowd, or to sit tight and hope that Luciano was intending to deliver them to the hotel in Palermo.

She'd had more than enough contempt for one day. Her eyes squeezed tightly as she struggled for self-control. Luciano drove along the cobbled road in a silence that she could have cut with a knife.

Steffy, who loved riding in cars, forgot his earlier bad temper and began to sing. His sweet little voice, chirping on merrily about the incey wincey spider, made her want to weep. Stealing a look at Luciano to see if he'd been softened by the touching little songs trilling from the back of the car, she saw that, on the contrary, Luciano's mouth had hardened and set like concrete.

'I don't want to talk to anyone. You've made it plain that you don't want me to *be* in Sicily, let alone talk to your family. So... you are going to let me escape from this madhouse, aren't you?' she mumbled anxiously to him.

'No. I can't.'

It was said softly and with a sinister curl of his lip. A shiver rippled through her and she deliberately had to quell the ridiculous fear that his dark clothes and grim manner had provoked. She wasn't in danger. Sicily wasn't all Mafia men and vendettas. What a stupid imagination she had.

'Why? I'm at a safe distance from your family now,' she said, failing badly to keep her voice from shaking. 'I'm sorry for the distress I caused and I'd give anything, *anything*, for it not to have happened. But I can't upset them any more. I'll forgo my visit to Gio's grave, I promise, if you'll let Steffy and me drive away and out of your lives.'

'Steffy?' He sounded disapproving.

'Stefano,' she explained.

He cursed under his breath as he temporarily lost control of the steering and the car swerved, grinding up the wild herbs by the roadside.

'I can't let you go,' he said grimly.

'You—you can't? Why——' she gulped '—why not? Not long ago you wanted me to keep a low profile.'

'But that was before anyone here knew you had a child,' he replied quietly.

Her hand flew to her heart in fear. Steffy. They wouldn't want her child, would they? They wouldn't take him away from her? 'That...that can't make any difference,' she rasped hoarsely.

'Oh, yes, it can. You *fool*,' he said with savage anger in every line of his face. 'As my mother said, we have business to discuss.'

'Like...what kind of business?' she asked warily, fidgeting nervously with the hem of her slim skirt.

'Family business.' He shot her a quick, contemptuous look. 'You'll have to face them. We don't have any choice in the matter.'

'I can't. You can't do this to me. I have nothing to say to your family, and I certainly don't want to listen to what they'll want to say to me. Please!' she begged desperately.

'You brought it on yourself. You had to come, didn't you?' he said savagely. 'You ignored everything I said! I warned you quite clearly that you risked trouble. Do you think I ever say anything for fun?'

'N-n-no,' she mumbled.

'I knew I should have bundled you off, the minute I saw you outside the church. I showed you too much pity.

Pia must have been looking out for you in that crowd of whimpering blondes,' he muttered angrily.

Stung by being bracketed with Gio's 'friends', Debbie frowned crossly. And then Luciano's words drove home. He seemed convinced that Pia had been on the alert for someone. An English woman.

'Our sandwich business,' she said shakily. 'Pia *was* deliberately trying to destroy it because——'

'Because you were Gio's woman,' Luciano finished coldly, his carved mouth etched with distaste. 'I worked that one out too. I don't blame her; I'd do the same. I'd never accept a rival.'

Debbie flinched at his condemnation but wouldn't remind him that it was Gio who'd been unfaithful. She'd been innocent. No one seemed interested in that fact. Her heart skipped a beat. 'Do you think she knew I had a child?'

Luciano scowled. 'I doubt it.'

She gulped, half afraid to ask her next question. 'Does . . . does she have . . . a child?'

Slowly, Luciano drew in a rasping, angry breath. 'No,' he muttered. 'She can't have children. And if she'd known earlier that you had a son she would have torn your eyes out with her bare hands.'

She shuddered, appalled at the angry passion that was bottled up in Luciano's powerful chest and suddenly uncomfortably aware of the intense passion that Pia must feel. Sicilian passion. Hot, fiery, deadly.

She stared ahead sightlessly. She'd crossed Luciano. Trouble was brewing. She was in a strange country amid hostile people. Pia was deeply hurt and would want to lash out. Whatever his feelings about the family, Luciano was furious with her for upsetting them at a painful time and presumably he set great store by his good name. Worse, Steffy was possibly in danger. Small shivers travelled down her spine. He must be protected at all costs.

'You're intending to take me to your house?' she asked jerkily.

The black brows jerked together. 'The House of the Lions. It was Gio's.'

Debbie gulped. That meant Pia owned it now. She didn't want to go there. 'Please don't,' she begged fervently. 'What is there to say? Nothing but insults. Why do you want me to be subjected to a slanging match? For Pia's sake? You want her to be given the opportunity to slag me off and tear my eyes out, while my son watches? For pity's sake, Luciano——'

'No, we're beyond pity,' he interrupted. 'You got yourself into this and now you have to face the music. I tried to keep it quiet, but everyone knows what your relationship was with Gio. They know you have a child who is Gio's heir.'

'Is that what's bothering you? We don't want anything from the Colleoni,' she cried heatedly. 'I told you, I'm not going to ask for anything. I want *out*, Luciano!'

'Tough.'

Her chest rose in exasperation. 'This heir business...you forget that Stefano is...illegitimate,' she said with difficulty, and went bright red with shame. She bit her lip and forced herself to continue. 'Surely Pia inherits Gio's estate, whatever that is?'

'I think the word "considerable" would describe it accurately,' drawled Luciano, slanting a sharp look at her. 'Still not interested?'

'No, of course not. All I want is to leave Sicily and never set eyes on the place again,' she said passionately.

'I doubt you'll want to, though no one will stop you,' said Luciano to her relief. He gave her a speculative smile that cut into her heart like a knife. 'You will have the choice. That would be only polite.' He paused, as if preparing to deliver a bombshell. 'But whatever you decide to do,' he said softly, 'the family will expect Stefano to stay here. He is a Colleoni and there will be opposition if you want him to return to England. The family will wish this to be his home now.'

CHAPTER FIVE

DEBBIE sat frozen with shock. Luciano wanted Steffy to live in Sicily? Over her dead body! She'd never agree to anything so bizarre. Steffy belonged in England, with her. Whatever was Luciano thinking of?

'Two liddle ducks dum dum dum day,' sang Steffy, blithely innocent of any danger.

She willed herself to speak but nothing happened. Her throat was locked up by the shock and by a terror that was twisting her stomach into knots. Common sense told her that she was being stupid; instinct whispered something else.

Panic-stricken, she saw that they had come to a set of wrought-iron gates which were opening automatically. This must be the house: high walls, several black-clad men hanging around and looking menacing in their slouch hats, rolled-up sleeves and dark sunglasses, a fierce-looking dog straining at a leash, barking at them.

Dear heaven, it was like something out of *The Godfather*! This might be Pia's home, but it was more like a fortress. More alarmed with every second that passed, she glanced back. Barbed wire on top of the wall.

A prison. Her fingertips touched her mouth as she gave a little gasp. Luciano scowled and she listened to Steffy's merry singing, waiting till she could control the wild beating of her heart and the tone of her voice.

'You can't imagine that you can keep Steffy in Sicily while I trot obediently home!' she managed at last, somehow sounding sharp and decisive.

'I've no idea what you'll decide to do.'

Debbie shook herself mentally. Luciano didn't realise how unrealistic he was being. 'This ... this idea is out of the question,' she squeaked. 'I'm not fooled by all this dark glasses and menacing stares bit! You're more English than Sicilian...'

'On the contrary,' he drawled. 'Since Gio's death, when I inherited the Colleoni estate, I've discovered my roots. I've learnt that I care about my heritage and that I have no wish to see it destroyed.'

Her mind digested that rapidly. 'You inherited it? Why not Pia?'

His dark eyes gleamed. 'Because the inheritance goes through the male line in our family. We thought that it was me; now everyone knows that Gio's son—bastard or not—is the true heir. Your son is the next Colleoni in line.'

'*Steffy*?' she cried, aghast. 'But he's just a little baby! And why are you being so noble-minded? Without Steffy, you can have it all. You don't want to lose the estate, do you?'

He stopped the car for a moment and flicked her a dark, speculative glance. 'No. Oh, no,' he said softly. 'I want the estate—I've always wanted it—and I know how to keep it.'

She shivered as his gaze raked her up and down as if she might be part of his plan, and cringed when she saw that with the anger, the single-minded determination in his eyes there was also sexual desire—so powerful that she felt the whole of her body acknowledge his masculinity by bursting into life.

'How?' she ground out, resenting her physical reaction to him.

'That is what we must talk about,' he murmured, holding her fascinated gaze with his. 'I want the land. I feel it should be mine,' he said, his mouth sultry as if he spoke of a woman he yearned for. 'All my life I've coveted it, dreamed of owning it. And for a short time, an unfairly short and tantalising time, it was mine.'

'You want it, you have it,' she cried, shaking off the languid warmth his voice and eyes had surrounded her with. 'I—I thought we were friends, Luciano.'

'Friends?' He studied her carefully, his eyes veiled. 'I . . . didn't think so.'

She flushed at her mistake. Of course. He was a rich aristocrat. A businessman. What an idiot she'd been.

'Let us go—we'll vanish. You can't want us to discuss this with your family. Steffy and I would threaten your position,' she argued frantically. 'Having Steffy around would ruin your hopes.'

'I don't think so,' he said calmly. 'I have every confidence in my strategies. If the first fails, I'll move on to the next.'

'What first? What next?' she demanded.

'Well . . . let's see,' he murmured.

With a very male self-assurance, he turned to her, his heavy eyelids dropping over drowsy, melting eyes, slowly lifted a hand, and pushed a strand of sun-shot hair from her cheek. His finger loitered there for a breathless moment, gently smoothing her peach-bloom skin.

It dismayed Debbie that she did nothing to stop him. He was menacing, of course—and she was scared for Steffy's sake. She blushed. No. Neither of those reasons. He had the power to capture her with his arrogant, masterful ways. And her own terrible desire for him aided and abetted his unwanted control over her common sense.

Somehow she forced herself to knock his hand away. Mutinously she scowled at his self-satisfied smile. 'I don't know what you're planning,' she snapped, 'but Steffy's going home and so am I. We live in England! My mother's there. I wouldn't dream of staying here.'

'Wait till we can talk properly,' he said smoothly, soothingly, as if to a fractious child.

'I don't believe this,' she raged.

'You will,' he replied grimly. 'I'm afraid you will.'

She drew in a shaky breath at the soft menace in his tone. He started the car up again and it purred down a long drive between narrow cypress trees formally edging the expansive, park-like grounds. The house was nowhere in sight.

The Colleoni had money—and money meant power, she mused anxiously, especially in a place like Sicily. If Steffy ever got into their hands and was taken from her, she'd almost certainly never see him again. She'd read of tragic stories in the newspapers where children of mixed marriages were involved in a dreadful tug of love.

This was a little different. Yet Luciano seemed determined to bow to his family's wishes and keep Steffy here. Her hands trembled. She had no idea how she could stop him from whisking Steffy away from her by force and bringing him up as his puppet. Luciano would have all the power and Steffy would be a mere mouthpiece, doing everything his uncle wanted.

A whimper filtered through her parched lips and she licked them so she could speak. Luciano mustn't know she was afraid of him. She had to pretend that she wasn't scared at all.

'Look, if we're a problem and a threat to your ambitions, surely you'll want us to...?' She almost said 'disappear'. She clamped her mouth shut on the word, alarmed at the thought. 'You'll want us to go,' she finished in a rasp.

'That's one solution,' he murmured, his voice unnervingly caressing. 'But my family will expect Steffy to stay, that's for sure. And they won't want you around.'

'That's ridiculous!' she exclaimed scornfully. 'I'm Steffy's mother. There's no way they can take him from me.'

'I hope it won't come to that, but there are ways,' he said confidently, his voice husky and low.

He gave her a faint, challenging smile and she frowned because she could think of a million ways: bribery, threats, absence, lies, brute force... Her breath caught in her throat at the thought of losing her son. She wanted to lean back and pick him up out of his seat and hold him so tightly that no one would ever be able to part them.

Yet she knew that all she could do in this land of private justice was to be cleverer than Luciano. She'd have to pretend to accept whatever he suggested and then seize the first opportunity to flee.

'I don't have any choice, do I? Whatever we do it must be done amicably,' she said, gathering some dregs of practicality together. She'd fool him with her amiable manner and cheat him of her son.

'Sure,' he said smoothly. He patted her shaking hands and suddenly squeezed them as if to reassure her. 'Don't worry. You'll like one of my suggestions. Trust me,' he murmured.

Trust him? How could she? And he'd sounded too plausible. He had too much to lose to waste time being charming and amicable. A fit of trembling kept her busy as she struggled to hide her fear from him.

The mansion had come into sight, a large and beautiful building reflected in a tranquil lake. Under any other circumstances she would have been delighted to visit such a lovely place. It was more like a *palazzo* than a villa— soft yellow walls, white stucco curls above the windows, plaster ribbons and swags above the huge double doors which were set at the top of a flight of marble steps. A huge place, large enough for ten wealthy families.

Wryly she thought of the tiny flat she had shared with her mother and wondered what Gio had made of it, with the cramped kitchen and the washing always hanging in the bath. She groaned inwardly in defeat. How could he have ever treated her seriously, how could he have seen her as anything but a casual fling, when he had had this to come home to?

She wriggled uncomfortably. 'This was Gio's house? The Villa di Leoni?'

'It was his from the day my father died ten years ago.' Luciano paused. 'It has been mine for a very short time and I want it for my lifetime.'

The pride and love in his voice were unmistakable. Steffy was threatening something Luciano cherished. And it sounded as if he wished the villa had always been his and never Gio's at all. His brother had been a rival. Debbie quailed. He'd hardly welcome his brother's son.

'See how beautiful it is,' he said softly.

'Gio had so much—a whole life I knew nothing about! I was nothing to him,' she said aloud, her eyes huge with misery.

'I wouldn't say that.' His unnerving gaze raked her from head to toe, his face quite impassive. 'I'm sure he found you irresistible.'

She didn't believe him, of course. Pia was more beautiful. Here there must be servants to make beds and do the ironing. Pia wouldn't be tired from housework. Her hands wouldn't look red and chapped, nor would she have short, practical nails.

'Not for long,' she said quietly. 'There were greater attractions here. He spent most of his life in this house with his legal wife, didn't he?'

'You wish he'd spent it all with you?'

Debbie thought she'd better not answer that. 'Don't you?' she retaliated, looking across at him from under her lashes. 'If he'd abandoned Pia for me, then you could have lorded it here, in his place.'

'I... I wouldn't have wanted that.' To her surprise, he was scowling at the beautiful mansion now as though he hated it... or hated the thought of losing it; she wasn't sure. Her heart thudded more urgently as she wondered how she could best protect Stefano. 'If I had, the whole Colleoni clan would have been without a home for the last ten years,' he drawled, equally evasive.

'Are you saying that you fell out with them ten years ago?' she asked in surprise. 'When your father died?'

He gave a short, mirthless laugh. '"Fell out". That's something of an understatement,' he said sardonically. 'I was eighteen when it happened. Everyone within earshot thought Etna had erupted. I was banished from the villa and from Castelleoni. And I will tell you later why that was,' he added, when she opened her mouth with that very question hovering on her lips.

'Where did you go?' she asked instead.

His face darkened. 'The streets of Palermo,' he growled.

Evidently it had been a harrowing experience which he had no intention of discussing for he immediately changed the subject.

'Well, Debbie, how strong are your feelings for your son? How much do you want to protect him—perhaps at the expense of your own safety?' he murmured silkily, but his eyes were calculating, as if he waited for her answer with some anxiety.

The car rolled to a sighing halt in front of the steps. 'I told you,' she said, her mouth feeling as if it was full of feathers, 'I'll guard him with my own life if necessary! I intend to stick close to my son, Luciano. And I'm relying on your love of children to make you think twice about tearing him away from me.'

Luciano's eyes lingered a little longer on her than she found comfortable. It seemed that he knew something she didn't and that infuriated her. 'He won't need tearing,' he said softly. 'And children are very adaptable to new situations.'

It was as she'd imagined—he meant to bend her son to his will. And he could, if she wasn't around. He'd draw Steffy like metal to a magnet. 'Don't try to manipulate him,' she warned darkly, quivering at the sinister force of his piecing gaze.

He smiled faintly and touched her face again. She should have drawn away but couldn't. To disguise the treacherous paralysis of her legs she gave him a haughty you-don't-scare-me stare.

'Shall I leave him alone and manipulate you instead?' he teased. And, to her astonishment, he leaned over and lightly kissed her full on the lips. 'I would enjoy that. I think you would too.'

Somehow she turned away, pride and sheer stubbornness preventing her from sighing at the sweet danger of his mouth. A kiss that tantalised. Left her longing for more. But she had to remember that he was playing a ruthless game. He wanted the inheritance and she knew he would climb mountains to get it. A kiss was no hardship to him if it meant she'd be intimidated and scared off.

'Do you think you can kiss me stupid?' she snapped.

'It's a challenging thought.'

She glared. 'Whatever high opinions you have of your technique,' she ground out, 'it won't soften my brain. I'm not leaving without my son,' she persisted doggedly.

'How tough you are.' He sighed, as if in pleasure.

'You'd better believe it,' she snapped, finding herself close to tears.

He'd changed. That was the reason for her misery. The prospect of the inheritance had soured the man she'd known in England. Upset by this, she watched with slate-dark eyes as three smartly dressed staff came running down the steps to greet Luciano. They opened the car doors with politely helpful smiles, as if being rich meant you were incapable of heaving down a handle and doing it yourself.

Behind her, she heard a man make a surprised comment and when she turned sharply she saw that he was undoing Steffy's straps. Quickly she leapt out of the car to do that herself.

'Horseys!' shrieked Stefano.

To her alarm, she saw that Steffy was perched on the shoulder of the middle-aged man who'd already released him from the car seat. The man laughed and put him down and in a flash Steffy was heading with all the determination of a steam train for the nearby field.

'Steffy!' she yelled frantically.

'Leave him,' ordered Luciano, his arm forming a barrier in front of her.

'Are you joking?' she seethed.

'Enrico will watch over him. He has children of his own—ten at the last count.'

'I don't trust you—or Enrico, however many children he has,' she snapped and ducked under his arm.

In two strides he'd caught up with her and grabbed her wrist, whipping her around to face him. 'You're being paranoiac,' he ridiculed.

She tossed her head so angrily that her hair flew around her face like a soft curtain. 'With your family around? Huh! I'm being careful. Let me go to my child,' she demanded, her eyes huge with fear and fury. 'My God, Luciano, you part me from him and I'll scream till your servants take pity on me and their eardrums and defy your orders.'

'You're not dressed for racing across fields,' he pointed out with infuriating truth.

She bent and snatched her shoes off with her free hand.
'Now I am,' she declared, flinging back her tumbled hair.
'Will you let me go to Steffy or do I create a scene you'll
never live down?'

'It's a tempting proposition. An Englishwoman, wild
with passion, abandoning her inhibitions to protect her
child,' he mocked. 'But you'd scare the horses. So...'

Debbie blinked, her heart turning over as she remembered her mother's remark, light-years ago, when she'd
rejected the idea of wearing the sprigged muslin. A
wistful tear rolled down her cheek for those days of
innocence.

Luciano's thumb flicked the tear away. 'Such passion.
Go, Debbie. You're free to go to your son,' he said softly.

Flinging him a contemptuous look, she ran after the
toddling Steffy and took his hand, leading him to the
post-and-rail fence. The horses came over inquisitively
and the two of them happily stroked the soft, snuffling
noses while she struggled to control her jitters.

It was an undeniably lovely setting, peaceful and
serene: fields and trees and meadows, silver-leaved olives,
rustling in the wind, the sound of a donkey clip-clopping
somewhere far away, the scent of thyme and oregano
and lavender drifting on the air as the sun released their
oils, and the unending whir of cicadas, easing her soul
and smoothing the furrows on her forehead.

If she could ride, she thought ruefully, she and Steffy
could leap on to the back of a horse and gallop across
the meadows till they came to the next village. She sighed.
If.

Steffy sat astride the fence, waving to the horses and
riding in his imagination. 'Horsey, horsey, hmm hmm
stop. Hmm hmm feet go cliply-clop...'

'Clippety,' came Luciano's velvety tones.

He came to stand behind her. Nothing more. But she
felt edgy at once as the hairs on her neck lifted and her

skin began to tingle. She could hear his breathing—heavy, like hers—feel each breath stir the hairs on the top of her head, anticipate it, shudder with its warmth.

Luciano stirred and she stiffened like a deer sensing danger. If only he'd say something! But he remained silent and she stood stiff as a board with tension, her eyes fixed on the far horizon where the sea glinted like a dazzling golden mirror.

At last, he spoke. 'Tell me, Debbie, do you like what you see?' he asked, his voice like a warm, murmuring breeze.

Slowly she turned her head, knowing he meant the scenery but thinking of what she was seeing now. And yes, she did. How could she feel otherwise? If she forgot the fact that Luciano was a threat, then she could admit that he was the most magnetic and good-looking man she'd ever seen, and that his powerful aura filled her with a strange energy which might be a promise of joy or passion or maybe just the knowledge that life with him would be living with a capital L.

He smiled, but not with his eyes, and she knew she'd been fantasising. The real man lay deep below the surface of this charismatic persona. Only his family knew what he was really like—and they didn't seem to like him at all.

'I can't think of anywhere more beautiful than this,' she said stiffly, pulling her mind back to the view.

Luciano's dark eyes gleamed. 'You must understand my feelings, then. People would kill for less.'

Her spine froze. 'Was that meant to be intimidating?' she challenged.

'It was an observation. I didn't mean it as a threat, Debbie.' He came to face her, giving her a long, searching look of such intensity that it made her knees go weak. 'When I was in London,' he murmured, 'I missed it here so much that it was like a physical pain in my chest. You know what I mean?'

'Yes,' she muttered, feeling that pain now and refusing to acknowledge why.

'I used to dream of it here,' he said softly. 'When the cornflowers colour the wheat fields, when the cistus blooms on the roadsides and the mimosa foams on the hillside, it's a magical place to be.'

'I thought... I thought at one point you looked at the house as if you hated it,' she said tentatively.

He was closer, a breath or two away, the warmth of his eyes mesmerising her, holding her entranced. 'I hate the memories locked up inside it,' he replied. 'But I want this place, this incomparable view, the scents, the sounds, the essence of what is Colleoni, with a passion I can hardly describe.'

She could see it. The fire heated him with such a force that it embraced her too, reaching out and searing her till she was breathless with its ferocity.

'You envied your brother,' she observed nervously.

'Gio?' Luciano's mouth curled in contempt. He was about to say something and then it seemed that he changed his mind, because his attention was caught by Stefano who was calling to the horses, now grazing a little distance from them. 'Would you like to ride the horse, Stefano?'

She frowned at Steffy's, 'Yes, please!'

'I don't think so. He's too little,' she said firmly.

But Steffy had held up his arms in excitement and Luciano was smiling at her son so tenderly that she felt her heart roll. He really did love children, she mused. And everything about the affectionate way he bent to her son suggested that he felt protective towards Steffy and would never harm him. So... what was his intention? To mould him in his image, as she'd thought earlier? Cold shivers rippled down her spine in icy waves and she clutched at her son's hand in fear.

'You come too,' Luciano suggested to her, stripping off his sombre jacket and slipping the gold links from his deep cuffs. His eyes were melting into hers, while his hands-on-hips stance challenged her. I dare you, his manner said. Show me you're not afraid.

But she was, and it irritated her that he'd promised something to her son without asking her permission first. There would be all hell let loose when she vetoed the treat.

'I—I can't, so he can't go either. Isn't that obvious? This skirt isn't suitable——'

'You can hitch it up. I'll get the horse, Stefano. Yes?'

'Yes! Yes!' squealed Stefano while, indifferent to her plight, Luciano vaulted the fence and a velvety chestnut came trotting obediently to his soft call.

She glanced back towards the house and saw that the family had emerged from the house and were watching them. It might have been her imagination but she was sure she could feel their hostility hurtling like flame-throwers in her direction. If she hitched up her skirt and showed her legs above the knee at a time like this they'd be horrified.

'I couldn't possibly,' she protested. 'It would be indecent.'

'Well, don't spoil Stefano's pleasure,' Luciano said lazily. 'He's about to burst at any moment.' Before she knew what he meant to do, he'd snatched the more than eager Stefano from her concerned grasp.

'Steffy,' she gasped in dismay. And, quick-thinking, she caught hold of the horse's halter as Luciano carefully placed Stefano on the chestnut's broad back. Now, she thought in triumph, he couldn't go anywhere.

'Look! Look, Mummy!' squealed Stefano, beside himself with glee.

'Stay very still,' warned Luciano, his right arm securely encircling Steffy. The little boy went rigid, only his eyes whizzing about his head in a comical excitement that had Luciano smiling in fond amusement. 'Now you, Debbie, and then I'll mount behind you.'

Was his purr suggestive? She wasn't sure; she only knew that she wasn't going anywhere if it meant being crushed to Luciano's body. And if she wasn't nor was Steffy. 'Are you crazy?' she protested. 'There's no saddle.'

'It's not essential.' The sexy note in his voice made her throat tighten. 'Personally, I prefer there to be no barrier between me and the feel of warm, shifting flesh.'

Debbie blushed. He *was* talking about something else! How dared he? 'I'm not letting you get your hands on me,' she said grimly. Let him make what he liked of that! 'You couldn't possibly manage the two of us.'

'I can do anything I want,' he said with unnerving confidence.

His gaze challenged hers and she knew he was referring to his plan. He meant to capture them both with his charm, his sensual skill, his sheer force of will. And she had to stop him.

'No,' she breathed.

He smiled winningly. 'Don't worry. I've ridden with a woman and child before so it's perfectly possible.'

She wasn't the first! A sudden pain shot through her body, making her draw in her breath sharply. A woman and a child. 'Who with?' she asked, blurting out the question with a force that surprised her.

'Enrico's daughter and her little girl. And Enrico wouldn't trust them with the Pope himself. So, you see, it's perfectly possible and perfectly safe.' Luciano's eyes mocked her predicament.

'Come *on*!' cried Stefano impatiently, bumping up and down till Luciano placed a staying hand on his chubby little leg.

'Wait. Your mother is deciding.' He turned to Debbie who was trying not to feel resentful because he could command instant obedience in her strong-willed son. 'You have a choice,' he said softly as she gazed earnestly at him, her dove-grey eyes wide with anxiety. 'Three choices, to be exact: to deny Steffy something wonderful and to keep him with you, to join him and me and enjoy the ride of your life, or to stay all on your own.' He smiled. 'What's it to be, Debbie? Which option do you choose?'

'I want to be with Steffy... and I want to stay down here,' she muttered, chewing her lip in agitation.

'If I've learnt anything in my life,' he drawled in amusement, 'it's that all choices have their advantages and their disadvantages. The trick is to weigh up which one is driven by the strongest passion and go for that whole-heartedly.'

'Mine is for my child,' she said crossly. 'So for his sake I'll have to suppress my loathing for you and risk making a spectacle of myself in front of your family.'

He beamed in smug satisfaction. 'They'll be appalled,' he agreed equably, as if he didn't care what they thought. 'But your son means more to you than your pride, or the fact that you'll suffer the scorn of others, doesn't it? I'm glad about that; he should come first. And, in the same way, my ambition means more to me than convention and seemliness, so don't imagine I'll ever act to appease others, Debbie. When I want something I go for it, whole-heartedly. No holds barred.'

'But we shouldn't be doing this today, of all days,' she objected.

He shrugged. 'We could be indoors, solemnly taking tea and sandwiches and talking quietly. But being re-

spectful to Gio won't help him now and I refuse to be
a hypocrite for anyone. I'd rather amuse a little boy—
and perhaps win a smile from his mother.'

He got a scowl instead. 'I hate you for making me do
this. It's under protest,' she muttered.

'I don't care how you're doing it,' he murmured, a
wicked gleam in his eyes. 'Only that you are.'

Luciano steadied Steffy and reached out an arm invitingly. Of course she didn't want to go, because she
knew it would be unwise. But what could she do?
Luciano fully intended to ride away with her baby
whatever she decided.

'You are a—a——' she stuttered, searching for the
right word.

Luciano found it for her. 'Bastard, so my mother tells
me,' he drawled. 'Get on, will you?' he said in amused
exasperation when she gaped. 'Or I'll jump up without
you and gallop across the fields.'

With his comment about his mother going round and
round her head, and encouraged by both Luciano and
the delighted Stefano, she reluctantly hitched up her skirt
and put her hand in his, blushing all the while as her
long legs were exposed. She placed her stockinged feet
on the rail and he helped her to climb to the top one
where she balanced precariously for a moment.

'What am I doing?' she grumbled to herself.

'Choosing with your heart,' he murmured. 'You can't
imagine how delighted I am.' He smiled at her puzzled
frown. 'Once committed, never falter,' he said huskily.
'Place one hand on the horse's back and leap up behind
your son; I will hold you. You won't fall; all the time
you must trust me.'

There was such a wealth of meaning in his words that
she imagined he was referring to far more than the horse
ride. She wanted time to think about this but he was
urging her on, making her continue what she'd started.

Tearing her eyes away from his with difficulty, she took a deep breath and leapt, feeling the supporting strength of his muscular arm. For a moment her legs hovered in mid-air and then they had slipped across the horse's warm back. She hugged Steffy to her in relief.

Luciano put one supple leather shoe on the rail and sprang up behind her, his sinewy forearms reaching around her waist. He settled himself close against her body.

'You hold on to your son, I'll hold on to you,' he said in a soft rush of warmth over her ear.

'Who holds on to the horse?' she asked grumpily.

'My thighs,' he said, and she felt their pressure, urging the horse into a gentle walk.

Steffy held his breath with excitement. She held hers because Luciano's body felt so hard—toned muscle shifting against her back with no barrier between them. Her gaze dropped to his hands which were positioned inches below her breasts and were forcing her firmly against him.

'Am I making you feel safe?' he enquired innocently.

Like hell! she wanted to answer, because her heart was leaping about frantically. Instead, she turned her head and asked a little breathlessly, 'You said your mother calls you a bastard. Is that an insult or a fact?'

'Both.'

She gasped. 'But you inherited the land...'

He leaned forward till his cheek touched hers and she couldn't pull away because he'd increased the pressure on her ribs. 'I told you, illegitimacy isn't important; the blood-line is. When Gio died, I was my father's only remaining male descendant. My existence was a source of great anger on the part of the woman I learnt to call Mother,' he drawled. 'It was bad enough that my father made her take me into his home and that she should have to treat his love-child like a son. It was even worse when Gio died and I took charge of the Colleoni estate.'

'Poor woman,' said Debbie compassionately.

'She'd be delighted to see me thrown out again,' he commented drily. 'Look between his ears, Stefano. Good. You can stroke his hair. It's called his mane.'

'Mane,' repeated Steffy, his voice filled with glee. 'Mane, mane, mane!' he cried, delighted with the new word.

Debbie was trembling. Luciano had kept his cheek against hers and it had no right to be there. The feel of his skin made it difficult for her to think. He turned his head so that his mouth was almost on hers and she sat there in frozen apprehension.

'However, I don't expect to lose my new home. I can avoid such a dreadful possibility. You see,' he said in a silken undertone, 'everything is possible if you want it enough.' When she slanted alarmed eyes at his, he smiled and shifted his hands a fraction higher so that she caught her breath in a terrifyingly delicious anticipation.

He wouldn't. He couldn't touch her breasts, she thought in panic.

'Hello, horsey, good horsey,' said Stefano affectionately, stroking the glorious long mane.

'That's right, he likes that. Well done,' approved Luciano warmly and Debbie felt her son stiffen with pride. 'His name is Nettuno—Neptune.'

'Would you move back a bit?' she asked coldly.

His mouth hovered centimetres away from her parted lips again. 'I don't think I should. I need to watch Nettuno's ears closely,' he said blandly, while she glowered into the mid- distance. 'He might get spooked by a snake. We can't risk us all falling off, can we?'

The warm fingers fanned out. His thumb was now lodged beneath the soft cushion of her breast and he must have known how rapidly her heart was beating.

'I think we've had enough,' she said.

'Oh? Do you want to get down, Stefano?' he said in surprise.

'No!' her son shouted emphatically.

'And nor do I. You've been outvoted,' said Luciano, sounding smug. 'Enjoy the experience. I am.'

'I bet you are,' she muttered, and gritted her teeth in frustration. This was the closest she'd ever been to such a virile male in the whole of her life and it disconcerted her. She felt horribly vulnerable. Luciano could do almost anything to her and she wouldn't be able to stop him because it would endanger Steffy.

With angry eyes, she surveyed the wild flowers and felt the weight of the heavy, heady silence of the heat of the day. In the quivering haze, purple clover fields stretched down the hillside. Small white villages glistened in a tumble of terracotta tiles and sturdy churches. Above their heads flew the screaming swifts and swallows, endlessly dipping and diving and making Steffy twist his head in amazement to see their antics.

'I can see islands out there,' she said brightly, diverting herself from her fears, and hoping she would divert Luciano, too. Because there was a hard rigidity pressing into her back and she could hardly mistake his arousal. His breathing had deepened. His body felt...more liquid—like hers. His hands were moving imperceptibly, with a maddening rhythm that seemed to cut off all the mechanisms that operated her brain.

'Isole Eolie—the Lipari Islands,' he murmured, the Italian words running seductively from his tongue.

She gulped. Of course he was feeling aroused. He was a man, wasn't he? A Sicilian, with an intensely passionate nature. What an idiot she'd been to imagine they were going to have a simple ride around the field.

Here she was, her skirt up to her thighs, hair loose, clasped to Luciano's body, his hands almost on her breasts. The sun was warm and adding to the sense of drowsy lassitude that permeated the shimmering air. His mouth nuzzled her hair and she started.

'The islands look beautiful,' she croaked, arching her body away.

'Stromboli to the right,' he said quietly, drawing her firmly back again. 'That pale blue cone, apparently floating in the silver sea. All these volcanoes...' he mused, the huskiness in his voice more pronounced. 'Dormant but simmering. Who knows when they might erupt?'

'Give me Southwark any time,' she said huskily.

'You're not *still* thinking of going home?' he asked sardonically.

'Of course! With my son! Steffy,' she said jerkily, 'I think it's lunchtime——'

'No! More!' he urged. 'Horsey, horsey, hmm hmm stop...'

Luciano joined in the nursery song, his deep rich tones surprising Stefano for a moment, and then the two of them sang cheerfully as he turned the horse and walked it back to the waiting family. They looked like black stone statues and just as welcoming.

Suddenly Debbie was mortifyingly aware of the picture they must present: a man and a woman and a child, she with ten yards of leg showing, he with his hands a fraction below the rise of her bosom. And not a wafer of daylight between them.

'You—you ought to hold me a little less intimately,' she said in strangled tones.

'Of course I should,' he said with the satisfied tone of a man who had the whip hand. 'But I won't. I wish to make a point to the family.'

'That I'm the kind of woman you can treat with contempt?' she snapped irritably.

'Don't compare me to my brother and how he treated women,' he countered.

Her eyes rounded and she whipped her head back in fury. 'I didn't mean that he'd behaved like that with me!' she ground out angrily.

'But that *is* how he treated you.' Luciano's hands tightened, crushing the breath out of her so she couldn't speak. 'So it's important that the family think I have claimed you as my own.'

'As your...*what*?' she gasped.

'It's the only thing they'll understand,' he drawled. 'You're obviously tainted in their eyes. They'd hardly expect me to treat you with deep respect under the circumstances. The only way I can protect you is to make them believe that I'm taking you over.'

CHAPTER SIX

'LUCIANO!' Debbie struggled to get rid of the rasp in her voice. 'You can't pretend any such thing!'

'But Stefano is at risk,' he said urgently. 'You and he must place yourselves under my wing or they'll destroy you both, one way or another. They won't dare to touch you if I'm in the picture. If they insult you, if they try to hurt you, they will have me to reckon with. Trust me,' he said again.

'Why?' she asked in confusion. 'Why should I? At the funeral you wanted me to hide myself away...'

'I told you,' he said patiently. 'I wanted to spare you the embarrassment of a public condemnation.'

'But... it doesn't make sense that you should want to protect me!'

'Not even for my own selfish reasons?' he said, amused.

'And what might they be?' she asked shakily.

His arm squeezed the breath out of her again. His mouth lightly touched her temple. And she felt fear and excitement mounting inside her. So all her concentration went on steadying her breathing and stopping her heart from pounding so fiercely against his sinewy arm.

'Patience, blind woman,' he chided. 'Enjoy the anticipation. For the moment, be glad that I'm taking care of you. They'd crucify you otherwise,' he drawled.

'They'll do that anyway,' she muttered.

'Brazen it out,' he urged. 'You did nothing wrong. If we stand together, with your innocence and my ruthlessness, they can't hurt you. Gio has left a tangle behind him.' Luciano's hand absently caressed Debbie's waist, the rhythm making her heart beat unbearably fast again. She looked down at the dark hairs on his arm in dismay, wondering why he affected her so strongly. 'It's going to take a while to unravel,' he whispered in her ear, 'and we want to decide what is best for Stefano.'

'To come home with me,' she said in panic.

'But remember,' Luciano said smoothly, 'the family will insist that he stays. He is a Colleoni.'

As if to emphasise that point, he stopped the horse a few yards from the fence. The house dominated her vision in all its grandeur, servants waiting to attend the waiting, apparently dumb-struck family, who were staring at her with total hostility.

Debbie picked out Pia and cringed back into Luciano's body. 'This is going to be awful! You say you'll protect me?' she asked, turning her head to look at him. He had taken care of her before. He'd been generous with his time, his concern. Hope flared in her heart, lighting her eyes.

He gave a faint smile and bent forward, his cool lips touching hers before she could withdraw. 'Kiss me back,' he said urgently. 'It's your only hope.'

'Wh—what? Why...?' she spluttered in confusion.

His mouth nuzzled her neck and she quivered. 'Because your mother's business will be ruined by Pia unless she sees that I am intent on taking care of you,' he murmured. 'Now turn back and kiss me. Save yourself from trouble and save your mother. Isn't that worth a kiss? Or are you afraid?'

'Of a kiss?' she said scornfully. 'Of course not.'

She should have been. Luciano's mouth was soft and yielding at first, then began driving against her with a passion she wanted to prolong because it salved her empty heart and helped her to release the stifled emotions she'd felt that day.

Pretending she was acting out the role he'd requested, she allowed his mouth to plunder hers, sinking beneath the sweet taste of his tongue that soon turned to something more sexual, more dangerous.

Her head whirled. Half fainting with dizziness, she groaned in his mouth and tore herself away. Seeing nothing, she felt Luciano's thighs tense, his heels urging the horse on. And when she finally focused she saw the contempt and hatred on every face that stared at her.

Had Luciano done that on purpose, she thought, to underline her cheapness? She groaned. She hadn't thought it through. She'd responded as she'd wanted to instead of as was wise. Fool, she castigated herself. Would she never learn?

'Let one of the men take the child,' Luciano said gently.

'No!' she snapped, holding Steffy tightly. 'No one's having him but me.'

'Whatever you like. Hold on. Don't fidget.' He slid lithely to the ground and held up his arms, his dark eyes goading her with their sardonic glint of amusement. 'Slip one leg over. I'll catch you both,' he said confidently.

Debbie bit her lip. Either she had to stay up there for eternity, or she'd have to fall into his embrace. Not much of a choice. Holding Steffy carefully, she eased one leg over to join the other and began sliding to the ground. Luciano's arms came securely around them both and she slithered down his body while Steffy squealed in delight.

Hot with embarrassment, she deposited Steffy on the ground and eased down her skirt. But the damage had been done, of course. Quickly she twisted her foaming blonde hair into a style that was marginally tamer and less abandoned and took her son's hand.

'That ride proved something important about your feelings towards me,' murmured Luciano, his eyes dark with secrets.

Heavens! she thought in panic. Had her attraction been that obvious? 'It proved something to me,' said Debbie quickly. 'You know all the words of "Horsey".'

He smiled. 'Evasive,' he said sardonically. 'I wonder why?' She set her mouth and refused to bandy words with him. He was a Sicilian and even better at it than a native East Ender. 'I think it was a very revealing episode all round,' he declared smugly. 'Ready for the family?' he enquired, lifting one wicked eyebrow.

Her sharp slate eyes clashed with his. 'Ready,' she muttered grimly.

Everyone watched Luciano gravely help the embarrassed Debbie to clamber back over the fence with as much dignity as she could muster. Her stockings had been laddered by the rough rails and she felt hot as several pairs of eyes homed in on the dreadful wiggly lines that drew the maximum of attention to her long legs.

'Isn't she *big*?' said the daintily elegant Pia acidly, in a whisper that could have reached Rome.

Mutinously, Debbie scooped up Steffy, who had crawled under the lowest rail, and stood defiantly returning the disdainful stares with a flash of her smoky eyes.

Luciano landed beside her with a sudden thud after leaping lithely over the fence. He put his arm around her shoulder and she knew better than to shrug it off.

'This, as you probably know, is the woman Gio cheated,' he announced ominously. 'Debbie...Baker. She and Gio went through a marriage ceremony——'

'So she says!' spat Pia.

'So my marriage certificate says!' countered Debbie robustly. 'So the registrar says!'

'And this,' continued Luciano, sounding as if he was enjoying himself suddenly, 'is Gio's son, Stefano.'

'Stef...' Gio's mother faltered, her hands fluttering at her dismayed mouth.

'It's the family name,' explained Luciano in a low aside, leaning close to Debbie. 'Given to the favourite son of the Colleoni.'

'But...Gio didn't have it!' she exclaimed, puzzled.

Luciano tapped his nose secretively. 'A source of anguish as far as the family is concerned,' he confided quietly. 'Especially as I was named Luciano Stefano. Now this,' he said more loudly, before she could get him to explain further, 'is Gio's mother. And this, as you know, is Pia. My father's brothers, sisters, their husbands and wives...their children. Shall we all go in?' he enquired.

Very much in command of the situation, he took her elbow and led her in. Trying to look as unconcerned as he, she heaved Steffy up uncomfortably on her hip because he was becoming such a dead weight.

'Let me take him.' Gio's mother was by her side, eyeing Stefano with wistful adoration.

'He won't go with you,' she said quickly, afraid of letting him go, and guiltily watched the woman's mouth quiver. This was his grandmother, she thought unhappily.

'He might,' suggested Luciano gently. 'And don't be afraid that my mother will drop him in a vat of boiling oil,' he added drily, seeing her reluctance. 'Can't you see she will be putty in your son's hands?'

The woman's dark eyes were begging her to part with Stefano. Cautiously, her good nature getting the better of her caution, Debbie held him out. To her surprise, her son beamed at his grandmother and then laughed when she made a funny face and took him in her arms. She began to exclaim how beautiful, how strong, how perfect he was and Steffy lapped it up. His father's son, Debbie thought wryly, and then bit her lip in shame.

They all marched into the entrance hall and then straight out again to a covered walk. It was like the cloisters in a monastery and ran right around a huge courtyard garden. Debbie realised that the house had been built to create this sheltered spot, with its softly burbling fountain and exotic plants. It was a perfect setting for the hundreds of strongly perfumed roses which filled the air with their powerful fragrance.

Pausing only to let Stefano splash his hands in the fountain under the indulgent eye of his grandmother, Luciano led the party through grandly carved doors and into a cool drawing-room. Debbie watched in awe as he calmly directed everyone to seats of his choosing; apparently everyone was equally in awe of him, for all meekly did as they were told.

So when he waved her to a seat next to a large brocade chair that was obviously intended for him Debbie deliberately walked to a window-seat because it was as far as she could get from him and the family.

He smiled faintly and sat down with all the authority of a prince, commanding everyone's attention by sheer force of his personality. 'I've asked you here because there are a few things I want to make clear,' he said crisply. 'We will behave in a civilised way and you will not abuse my hospitality——'

'This isn't your house any more!' snapped Pia.

'We have several things to establish,' he acknowledged quietly. 'Until we do, we must assume that it is.'

'It's Stefano's house!' cried Gio's mother, clasping Steffy to her bosom. Debbie's eyes narrowed in alarm till she realised he'd wriggle free and felt a great relief when he did. 'And I'm his grandmother, so *that* woman,' she snapped, pointing at Debbie, 'she——'

'Take care,' warned Luciano softly. 'Debbie is his mother. I don't expect you to offend her. Go down that road and you'll find yourself out on your ear. I think we'll all have a drink, collect our thoughts and then I will explain how I see the situation. Vittore!' he called.

While the stiff-backed Vittore took everyone's order, Stefano began to wander around, enthusiastically examining decorative objects on the graceful occasional tables which were probably 'Louis the Something', if only she knew.

Seeing Steffy's hand hovering over a decorative teapot that looked as if it might be Chinese and madly valuable, she half rose in alarm, but Luciano had got to the table first and squatted down, shaking his head in a gentle warning.

'We must be careful of the teapot because it might break,' he said solemnly.

Steffy's eyes widened and he hastily tucked his little hands out of harm's way under his armpits. Debbie heard the audible sigh of amused affection roll around the room and she relaxed a little, smiling lovingly at her son.

'Shall we see what's painted on the teapot?' suggested Luciano.

'Flowers,' Stefano pronounced.

'And those are dragons. And there—is that a lady having tea?' His long finger pointed and Stefano respectfully peered closer, enthralled with the scenes.

'Liddle boy!' exclaimed Stefano, pointing with a carefully restrained finger.

'So it is. What's that in his hand?' murmured Luciano.

Steffy jumped up and down. 'Frog,' he cried excitedly, remembering his favourite animal book. 'Hop, hop, hoppy hop!'

'Steffy, careful,' warned Debbie anxiously, seeing that he was about to perform frog-leaps on the spot.

'Look at this,' Luciano said quickly, deftly moving the fragile teapot away and placing a button-hook in Stefano's hands. Debbie grinned to herself. Luciano must know that small children couldn't do too many things at once. Looking and holding and being intrigued meant no jumping and squealing. 'This,' he said gravely, 'is for doing up the tiny buttons that your grandma's mummy had on her dress.' He turned away and secretively flicked open the buttons of his waistcoat to reveal a gold satin lining. 'But maybe we can do mine up with it. What do you think? You help me.'

He'd handled the situation brilliantly. He'd used her trick of defusing Steffy's stubborn insistence on examining an object to his entire satisfaction by introducing something more interesting. Clever, she thought wryly, and wondered if he did that with adults too.

Luciano and Steffy were absorbed in trying to pull the waistcoat buttons through. A touching sight—two sets of impossibly long black lashes lowered in grave concentration. Child and man united. It was charming and tugged at her heart.

Her eyes flicked to the rest of the gathering. Gio's mother was looking sentimental, like everyone else. Or nearly everyone. Pia looked murderous, and caught Debbie watching her.

'It's a button-hook,' she said unnecessarily.

'I gathered that,' retorted Debbie, stung.

Pia sniffed. 'Late nineteenth century. I don't suppose someone like you would even know the period of this house.'

'No, I'm ignorant of things like that,' she admitted. Was it eighteenth century or nineteenth? Her soft grey eyes studied the graceful proportions, the crystal chandelier and the frescoes on the wall. Beautiful. The paintings and the silver must be priceless. 'Does it matter?'

'Does it *matter*?' Pia shuddered, her eyes rolling to the ornate plaster ceiling. 'God! How could Gio——?'

'He did!' said Luciano sharply. 'Remember Debbie's feelings. That should be the end of it.'

Pia scowled. 'He loved this house,' she said fervently. 'Its history, its ambience... He knew every item in it— and its value! She's just an ignorant little tramp more used to karaoke than *La Traviata*.'

'*La Traviata*,' mused Debbie pleasantly, managing to keep her temper. 'Is she a friend of yours?'

'She's taking a rise out of you,' drawled Luciano when Pia looked shocked. 'And don't pretend that you enjoy opera. Beyond the popular arias you get just as bored with it as I do.

'I think we really ought to get down to business. For Debbie's sake and Pia's, I will outline the situation of the inheritance. Then no one will be in any doubt as to the legality of Stefano's position.'

'I'm Gio's widow!' snapped Pia, her mouth a dark scarlet slash in her beautiful face. 'You said yesterday that I was to be looked after.'

'That goes without question,' acknowledged Luciano gravely. 'You inherit his trust fund, in accordance with your wedding-day agreement.'

'And you get nothing,' smirked Pia triumphantly.

'Perhaps I should explain,' said Luciano, seeing Debbie's puzzled frown. 'On Gio's death, I inherited the whole estate. Most of you know that in our family if the first son dies without a son and heir the second son inherits. However, there has been a new development. Gio does have a son——'

'A bastard!' spat Pia.

'Maybe,' agreed Luciano equably. 'But whatever his legitimacy there is no doubt that he is Gio's son. Therefore I no longer inherit the estate. Stefano is the heir and must be brought up accordingly.' He beamed

at everyone but Debbie felt that his grin was forced and
her heart fluttered in alarm. He didn't mean it. He was
plotting something. 'Agreed?' he asked genially.

'No,' she said firmly. 'We want to go home.'

'You go,' agreed Gio's mother eagerly. 'Leave. We
don't need you. We can bring Gio's son up to be a true
Sicilian, a true Colleoni,' she said proudly.

'I can't leave him!' cried Debbie, shocked, feeling as
if events were overtaking her. 'You want me to abandon
my child?'

Luciano stood up, his dark eyes sweeping the whole
gathering. 'If anyone is to bring Stefano up, it will be
me.'

'But you are——' Gio's mother clamped her mouth
shut at Luciano's angry jerk of his head in her direction.

'I am my father's son,' he said softly. 'I have his blood,
I had his love—and I have the Colleoni name.'

Debbie tensed at the cold hostility between them. There
was a terrible atmosphere of hatred and bitterness that
she wanted to escape. 'I am bringing Steffy up,' she said
rebelliously. 'In England.'

'We will see,' Luciano said confidently. 'We will talk
about this, just you and me. Your son has an inheritance,' he reminded her, an alarmingly insincere smile
on his face. 'You can't deprive him of it.'

'I could,' she said in agitation. She frowned. Her flight
was tomorrow and her mother was expecting her back.
'I can't change my travel plans just because it suits you,
Luciano,' she pointed out sharply.

'I'll persuade her to do the right thing, don't worry,'
he said to his worried-looking family. And they were so
confident in his ability to do so that they all visibly relaxed. 'Debbie, will you agree to staying on for a few
days?' he enquired with velvet charm. 'You can't object
to that, surely, when there's so much to discuss? A few

days,' he coaxed. 'It would be churlish of you not to agree.'

'I can't.' She frowned.. 'My ticket runs out tomorrow and I have to get back to work.'

'If you're worried about the business, my secretary will arrange for your mother to be given some expert emergency assistance,' Luciano said smoothly. 'You will telephone your mother and tell her what has happened. Nothing about the inheritance, of course—that must stay a private matter for the moment; but she won't begrudge you a few more days here, will she?'

'She might,' Debbie murmured, knowing perfectly well that she wouldn't.

'You have to agree, Debbie. You owe your son this. A few days of your time. If I can't persuade you in that time...well, I'll have to accept your decision, won't I?' He fixed her with his irritatingly intense gaze.

'I don't trust you,' she said sullenly.

'Very wise,' he approved. 'But look at it this way. I'm only asking for a mere moment in terms of Stefano's future—and he deserves your concentrated thought on this, not some hasty, emotional decision.'

She bristled. 'I'm not hasty and——'

'And us?' demanded Gio's mother, the set of her mouth ominous.

'You will not set foot on this land without my permission,' Luciano answered with soft savagery. 'Until the decision is made, I call the shots.'

Debbie opened her mouth. 'What about me? I'm——'

'And me?' pouted Pia. 'Where am I to live? You said I could have the east wing.'

'I suggest you stay elsewhere for the next couple of days.' Luciano's tone was so decisive that it made the suggestion sound like an order. 'After that...' his mouth curled in contempt '...you'll have enough money to buy yourself some history of your own, Pia.'

'You want me out of the way while you try her out?' she sneered.

'How dare you?' cried Debbie indignantly.

Luciano's gaze pressed her back into her chair. 'She's under my protection,' he said, cold steel lacing his tone. 'We all know what that means. No one can harm her and I cannot touch her.'

'But you're not a man of honour,' said Gio's mother, white-faced.

There was a gasp from all around the room as Luciano drew in his breath at the insult. Debbie quailed at the crackling fury in his eyes. But she knew that such a proud woman would never have made such a terrible slur on his Sicilian honour if it hadn't been true. And if it *was* true, thought Debbie in alarm, then she was in trouble!

'I suppose you considered Gio to be honourable,' said Luciano in a soft, dangerous growl.

'He was ten times the man you are!' declared Gio's mother, jumping to her feet.

Upset, Debbie glanced up at the ominously still Luciano. Some things were being explained. There *had* been a rivalry between the brothers. Gio had been the favourite, perhaps because of the circumstances of Luciano's birth. She remembered that Luciano had only been turned out of the house when he was eighteen—when his father had died. That wasn't unreasonable. Gio's mother must have been a saint to have brought up her husband's bastard.

And Luciano had resented his half-brother. He'd envied Gio's position as heir to the estate. There had been that terrible quarrel when Luciano had been thrown out on his ear by the family. So now he was taking his revenge, grinding their noses in the dust, using the power he could now wield.

'I refuse to be drawn on my feelings about my brother,' he said stiffly.

'Huh!' scorned Gio's mother. 'You've slandered him often enough in the past, though. And he was an innocent.'

'Gio was a bigamist,' Debbie said suddenly, wanting to put the record straight—and then wondered why she'd done so.

'Thank you, Debbie,' Luciano drawled, his eyes still lashing his family with an anger that was close to erupting and spilling out in a destructive stream. 'I'm grateful to you for pointing out the fact that Gio wasn't perfect. None of us is and it's a mistake to put anyone on a pedestal and worship them. I don't want to discuss Gio. This is not the day for going over old ground. I've told you what I'm going to do and now you will leave. My secretary will telephone you with Debbie's decision once it's been made. Vittore will show you out.'

He sat down again, his regal manner compelling everyone to rise in shocked silence. But perhaps Pia had more to lose and so dared to risk Luciano's wrath, because she came over to Debbie and stood in front of her, an expression of utter scorn on her face.

'He thinks in a few days he can sweet-talk you into doing whatever suits him,' she said nastily. 'But remember this: Luciano has hungered for the Villa di Leoni all his life. He has coveted it so much that he hated Gio and told terrible lies about his brother because he stood in his way.'

Shocked, Debbie slanted a glance at Luciano, who was lounging unconcerned in the chair, his mocking eyes fixed on Pia as if it made no difference whatever she said.

'And now,' continued Pia viciously, 'just when he thinks he can lord it over everyone here, his brother's bastard turns up to take the Villa and all the land from him. Use your brain, you stupid fool! Luciano has no morals or mercy and he obeys no laws but his own. Do you really think he's going to stand by and let that happen? Aren't you afraid for your child? For yourself? God help you, Luciano will drag you down to the gutter like all the other women he——'

'Enough!' It was quietly spoken, but the warning was unmistakable—Luciano had reached the end of his tether.

'I think it is,' agreed Pia tightly.

She turned on her elegant heel and stalked out while Debbie stared after her in horror. The heavy door closed and she and Luciano were alone, with her child—the child who would prevent Luciano from possessing something he had longed for all his life—bouncing merrily on Luciano's knee.

'Steffy,' she said, keeping her voice level, 'come here, darling. Mummy has something to tell you.'

'No,' he answered, shaking his blond head. 'Bouncin'.'

'You can bounce on my knee,' she offered shakily, flushing at Luciano's amused look. 'Or we can play 'Row, row, row the boat'. How about that?'

'No,' persisted Stefano. 'Bouncin'.' He beamed at Luciano.

'I want you to understand,' murmured Luciano, 'that I am totally in control here. We will discuss what is to happen courteously, but I will end up getting what I want in the end.'

'And what is that?' she asked nervously.

His slow, secretive smile mesmerised her. 'I want so much,' he said huskily. 'Where do I begin?'

'You can have it all! The house...'

'Yes.'

'The land...'

'Yes.' The black eyes mocked her alarm. 'Perhaps more, a lot more.'

She digested that news and wondered if she was imagining it, or if there had been a sexual meaning in that huskily spoken 'more'.

'Let Steffy come to me,' she said shakily.

'No. He's happy with me.' The mouth curved into a sinister smile again and her hand flew to her heart in terror.

'You—you'd use a child—blackmail me by... by threatening Steffy—to get what you want?' she demanded hoarsely, her temper rising—a temper that was slow to burn but was burning almost uncontrollably now. If he ever tried to harm one hair of Steffy's head...

'Be grateful to me, Debbie,' he said smoothly. 'I got the family off your back, didn't I? They could have reduced you to floods of tears if I'd let them'. Your self-respect would never have recovered—and it wouldn't have been something you'd have liked your son to witness.'

'You didn't do that for me. You wanted to get rid of them for—for whatever you want to do,' she muttered, wondering if she could race over and snatch her son away. She calculated the distance, the amount of energy needed to keep going and hurtle through the doors and run like hell.

'Partly true,' he agreed equably. But his eyes gleamed—with desire or intrigue? She didn't know. She only knew that her heart was beating fit to leap from her body. 'You see, I need some uninterrupted time with you.'

She licked her dry lips and her nerves shimmied in a distracting dance all through her body when his eyes followed the movement and warmed to it, becoming as drowsy as she was feeling now. As sensual as... Oh, God! she thought wildly. What's happening to me?

'Sossergiz,' said Steffy hopefully.

Startled, Debbie composed herself with difficulty and checked her watch. 'Oh, darling, it's way past lunchtime,' she cried guiltily. 'I have to do him something,' she said to Luciano. 'His favourite is sausage and mash but...'

He uncoiled from the chair like a springing panther. 'We'll go to the kitchen. Stefano can choose something for himself and watch his lunch being prepared.'

He reached for Steffy's hand and, much to Debbie's resentment, her son trustingly placed his small paw in his. The two of them walked amiably to the door, discussing the merits of fat or thin 'sossergiz'. With a sigh, feeling rather left out, she followed in their wake.

Surprisingly, lunch was rather fun. Outside the kitchen on the terrace, beneath a shady canopy of vines, they ate with several staff who took great pains to entertain Steffy, and Debbie reflected that it was a long time since she'd actually eaten a whole meal before it congealed on her plate.

Normally she'd be seeing that Steffy ate properly and it was a real treat not to bolt her food but to savour it, especially the home-made pasta and the wonderful cheese. Stefano took to the strange food like a duck to water and she wasn't sure whether to be glad or sorry.

'He'll need a sleep,' she said uncertainly afterwards, seeing Steffy's eyes drooping in the warm air.

Maria had already noticed. The cook had gathered the drowsy child up and pressed him to her ample bosom while she sang a lullaby to him. They all watched as her son struggled to keep awake and Debbie smiled tenderly when he failed and the heavy lashes became still at last.

'*Bello, bello*,' smiled Maria fondly and Debbie bathed in the sunshine of everyone's admiration for her son.

'We'll take coffee in the drawing-room,' said Luciano decisively, rising from his seat at the head of the table, 'and make arrangements for your luggage to be brought here. And I think you should make a telephone call to your mother and tell her you won't be coming home tomorrow.'

Debbie met his eyes in defiance. 'I'm not leaving Steffy for one minute,' she said flatly.

'We'd better send out for some glue,' he said drily.

Debbie kept her gaze level. 'I mean it.'

'Then Maria must come with us.' He said a few words to the surprised Maria and the three of them made their way back to the elegant salon where Luciano settled Maria on the veranda, then extracted the name of Debbie's hotel from her and arranged for a driver to fetch her things. 'Please sit,' he said, waving her to a brocade chair.

'What money will do,' she marvelled wryly, astonished by the rapidity of Luciano's decisions and the speed with which everyone obeyed him. 'It eases life no end.'

He shot her a sharp look. 'I'll give you money, Debbie. More than you've ever dreamed of. Perhaps we should get down to business. I have a couple of scenarios in mind. First, my family's preferred option: that you go home with a generous settlement from me, and I will bring Stefano up to be my heir——'

'*No*! No, no, no, no!' she cried, her nails dragging into the soft brocade.

'Well, bear it in mind,' he said, not at all discomfited. 'Let's try another one. You keep Steffy with you in England. Now, if you really feel you must take him home, then I'll settle fifty thousand a year on you. Think of it; you needn't work any longer. It's not good that a mother of such a young child should work.'

'Some of us have to,' she said in a matter-of-fact tone. 'And I don't need your money. Steffy's very well catered for at the nursery.'

'But it would be better if you didn't work, wouldn't it?' he argued with quiet persistence. 'And with fifty thousand wisely invested your mother needn't work either. You can stay in the same area, where you're comfortable and happy——'

'And you're saying that you'd really let me take Stefano home—and pay me to do so?' she asked, stunned by the offer.

'Of course.' He gave her a calculating look. 'Naturally you would waive his rights to the Colleoni estate on his behalf.'

'Naturally,' she said, the penny dropping. 'I'm to sell Steffy's birthright to you!' Luciano inclined his head in mocking agreement. 'You deceived your family,' she accused. 'You pretended to them that you wanted Gio's son to inherit, whereas you were really waiting for the chance to buy him out.'

'Correct.' Nonchalantly he crossed one leg over the other.

She glanced towards the veranda and saw that Maria was deeply asleep, snoring gently but still safely cradling the precious bundle in her arms, so she lowered her voice to a hoarse whisper.

'You knew your family would stick up for Stefano's rights come hell or high water, so you decided to get rid of them. And you were sure you could persuade me to surrender those rights on Steffy's behalf.'

'Correct again.' He gave her a warm and winning smile. 'And you want to go home, don't you? You'll be back in the bosom of your family, with everyone who loves you. I know how important that is to you, Debbie. And yes, I envy you that love. It's not something you should lightly throw away. I expected you to choose to take Steffy home, not because that suits me best, but because that's where your heart lies. You follow the dictates of your heart. I learnt that on our ride together. I'm right, aren't I?'

'Yes,' she said, feeling a sudden wash of misery flowing through her, making her want to cry. She wanted to go. He wanted her to go too, and that upset her, she thought, astonished that she should be so contrary.

'It's a good decision; you'll be comfortably off, I'll have the estates. Can we do business on those lines?' he asked huskily.

She hesitated and Luciano's suave, deceptively amiable expression grew watchful. Doubts began to crowd her mind. In this house she'd be a fish out of water, but Steffy was young enough to adapt. Legally it *was* his house. Could she deprive him of a wonderful lifestyle, a childhood of ponies and comfort, a good education and a financially certain future?

On the other hand, could she live without him? Of course not. And she was torn between love and duty. To sit on the fence with Steffy, or to let Steffy ride the horse. But...why change the order of things, when Luciano was obviously so well-suited to running the Colleoni estate? Because Stefano would never forgive her when he found out, she thought.

Her pained eyes met Luciano's. 'I don't know. I don't know what to do.' She drew a hand over her forehead. 'I'm tired and not thinking straight. It's not the best time to make such an important decision.'

'Perhaps. But the sooner you go, the safer you will be,' he said softly.

Rigid in the chair, she asked warily, 'You're actually suggesting that I'm not safe here?'

He gave a low laugh. 'I'm not going to strangle you, or plunge a dagger in your heart. I was thinking of the sexual danger you're in. You see, Debbie, I find you overwhelmingly attractive and I'm finding it harder and harder to keep my hands off you.'

She was shocked into silence. To her shame, his announcement had left her quite breathless. There was no doubting the danger, but there was an unholy excitement fizzing in her veins too. With difficulty she suppressed it and fumbled for some put-down remark.

'Well!' She moistened her lips. 'You find me attractive?' she echoed stupidly, playing for time. She saw his eyes on her body and had a brainwave. 'Despite my cheap suit?' she asked sarcastically.

'Please!' he demurred. 'Give me credit for seeing beneath the clothes.'

The way he was looking at her, she could well believe that he could do such a thing. Never before had a man's eyes told her so much or done so much. Her skin tingled with unwanted life, her pulses seemed intent on deafening her, and as for breath...

She had to escape from the house. Luciano had to leave the room some time. When Steffy woke, she'd take one of the cars...

'I hope you're not thinking of leaving us?' he enquired, and smiled at her guilty jump. 'This place is seething with alarms. My men patrol the grounds with dogs. At night, if you step one foot outside your bedroom door then all hell is let loose.'

'That must cut down the bedtime activities of your guests,' she muttered petulantly.

'I wouldn't know,' he drawled. 'I only had the system installed yesterday. You're my first guest since I took over on the day that Gio died. There was no alarm system when *he* was here, of course,' he reflected scathingly. 'Too inhibiting.'

'Why "of course"? Inhibiting what? What are you implying?' she asked warily.

'I leave it to your common sense to work out. I've long ago given up trying to tell people what Gio was like. I doubt you'd hear a word against him. You were his common-law wife and you loved him once. But you must know what he was by now.'

'You—you're suggesting he was promiscuous,' she objected.

'The evidence is there,' he drawled, though bitterness underlined each word. 'What do you want—diagrams?'

She went over and hit him, hard on the face—something she'd never done before, something she never wanted to do again because she felt so awful.

He must have seen it coming, yet he did nothing to stop her, just brought his head back after the stinging blow and continued to gaze at her steadily, a wealth of knowing in his dark eyes, a light of triumph telling her that her reaction betrayed her fear that he was speaking the truth.

And then he reached up with his arm, bringing her head down quickly before she could slip away. And he kissed her. Beautifully. With a slow seduction of her mouth that made her knees tremble. 'Don't waste your time and energy on a man who was not worthy of you,' he said quietly, releasing her all too soon.

She wiped her shaking hand across her mouth, her eyes blazing above it. 'You're jealous of him,' she whispered angrily. 'Gio was adored by everyone, wasn't he?'

'Oh, yes,' Luciano said coldly.

Bright colour flamed in her face, almost as deep as the mortifying mark of her hand on his cheek. 'And you hated him for that,' she declared. 'He always had an irresistible little-boy appeal...'

'You said it,' he drawled coolly.

'Damn you, Luciano!' she flared. For a moment she faltered. Luciano wasn't a little boy at all; Luciano was all man—not smooth and soft like Gio, but strong, with a rough edge and a steely determination which had been shaped by hardship. She could imagine it: the streets of Palermo, poverty, the need to survive by sheer cunning alone, the climb to success, achieved by ruthlessly stamping on anyone in the way...

She couldn't help but compare the two brothers. The differences between them were so remarkable that it was unavoidable. One had been handed a silver spoon, the other nothing, not even family love, apparently. One had grown up to be indulged and spoilt, the other had made his own good fortune by the sweat of his own brow. Gio had been soft in comparison. And selfish, she had to admit it.

Was that what happened to rich children who were denied nothing? It was a lesson, surely, because she wanted Stefano to be more like his uncle. Not like his father. She trembled at the discovery and blinked at Luciano, sitting there with so much explosive male energy, and she scrabbled around in her brain for the thread of her argument while he continued to watch her with his wicked damn-you-to-hell eyes.

'What are you thinking?' he murmured softly.

'Of Gio!' she flung.

With a muttered curse, he drew her to him again, sliding her on to his lap. And he kissed her as she'd never been kissed before, hard, punishing kisses that bruised and satisfied her in equal measures. She felt herself melting in his arms, beginning to respond. And self-preservation made her struggle even though her head was whirling with excitement and Luciano's deep, slow kisses were arousing her unbearably.

At her first push against his broad chest, he drew back and she unwound her arms from his neck then stood up, blushing a rich beetroot.

'You—you're trying to manipulate me,' she complained shakily.

'Yes.' He smiled at her gasp. 'But I'm only being straightforward and honest about my intentions and my feelings,' he protested, opening his hands in a gesture of hurt innocence.

'By telling me you find me attractive?' she flung, upset that for him it was all a game when her body was pumping with unfulfilled hunger.

'Oh, it's more than that.' Luciano's slow and languorous gaze riveted her to the spot. 'You know it, I know it.'

'Know...what?' she demanded nervously, her lips parting with the shallow breath that caught her body in a turmoil of confusion.

There was a long silence. They were so close that they could touch one another and the urge for her to do so—to place a hand on his broad chest and deliver herself to his arms for a taste of his lips again—was so strong that she had to concentrate fiercely to save herself from any such stupidity.

Warmth suffused every inch of her flesh, every vein, each nook and cranny of her body, especially those nooks she'd prefer to remain on ice. Hot flushes, she told herself, hoping to be amused. And gloomily she wished they were.

She couldn't stop what was happening to her any more than she could stop a Chieftain tank by sheer will-power alone.

Something terrible had happened when she'd first set eyes on Luciano. An irresistible call to her heart. A terrible helter-skelter tumble into unwanted and uncontrollable longing for something she couldn't—shouldn't—desire.

Luciano.

She'd never wanted anyone like this before. She didn't know what it was that she felt for Luciano, only that it was overwhelming and quite without sense or reason and she'd never been so scared or so exhilarated in her life. If Luciano hauled her into his arms one more time, she'd be helpless. And it would only take a few moments before

her caution and sense of decency would be thrown to
the winds.

Her mother had fallen for her father like that. Bang!
her mother had said. Like being hit with a knock-out
punch by a bare-fisted boxer. Was it happening to her?
Or did she yearn to replace Gio's part-time loving with
something infinitely more powerful?

Incapable of helping herself, she found that her eyes
were fixed on Luciano's achingly masculine mouth.
Sultry curves, as if chiselled by an angel in stone. His
lips promised those kisses which would be hard and firm
and dry and would have the power to obliterate the
outside world. Hell! Her mind was stuffed with wool!

Wrong time to make any major decisions. Unwise to
leap in any direction, particularly where her wounded
emotions were concerned. No, she must be calm and
sensible and think only of Steffy's welfare and safety.

'You're deliberately trying to scare me so that I'll run
away,' she said hoarsely, her grey eyes enormous and
glistening.

'I'm trying to warn you of what might happen,'
Luciano corrected her softly. His eyes seemed to melt.

Slowly he reached out for her limp hand and brought
it to his mouth. Then he jerked her forward so that she
was bending over him. She could have moved, should
have moved. He wasn't holding her that tightly. But she
remained there, her warm breath mingling with his, her
lips parting as her chest tightened with a terrible sexual
ache.

If she called out, Maria would wake. But she allowed
Luciano to seduce her with his satanic black eyes. And,
encouraged by her lack of resistance, his lips took on a
sultry smile while his free hand slid towards the V of her
jacket. She gave a little gasp as his fingers drifted lightly
over her satin-smooth skin. Some wickedness was urging
him to probe lower, to stroke the curve of her breast and

dip deep enough to cup the fullness of each straining globe.

'Warning?' She mumbled the word, incapable of doing anything else.

Luciano's lips parted to reveal his perfect white teeth. 'I like to warn women I desire that they risk seduction if they encourage me,' he said huskily. 'It only seems fair and honourable to give them the chance to walk away untouched if that's what they wish. So I thought you ought to know that if we both stay here tonight I'll do everything in my power to bed you.'

CHAPTER SEVEN

LUCIANO meant every word. A thrill of fear scurried through Debbie's veins, heightening the hot, giddy feeling that threatened to destroy her wits. Power surged from him, enwrapping her. Her skin tingled from the electricity that crackled from his eyes. Even when perfectly still, his energy surged and throbbed in his body like a dynamo. Such power was compelling. Dizzy with it, she stared at his bared arms, seeing the strength in them, her foolish mind imagining them around her, holding her all night...

'You haven't answered. I imagine that that's feminine modesty. Will you be waiting for me in your room?' he murmured. His lazy gaze wandered over her body till her throat dried. 'You are very tempting. Erotic. I want you. I really want you, Debbie.'

Terrible things were going on in her body. Shameful, primitive things. And she had to stop them. Steffy, she thought, brutally bringing herself to her senses. If she went soft and submissive, there was no knowing what would happen to Steffy. *This* kind of treatment she found difficult enough to deal with; threatening her son was another matter entirely.

'You'd change your mind if you saw my flannel nightie,' she said with a bold, bright defiance, and felt a little better.

Luciano laughed and his laughter stopped her recovery in its tracks. God, he was good-looking. Hardly surprising that her heart had tumbled and fluttered inside her body like a whirling postcard rack. She was silly and vain. The flattery had been balm to her wounded pride.

'You forget,' he said in amusement, his eyes crinkling in an unfairly appealing way, 'I've seen you in fancy dress, a shapeless cardigan and nondescript jogging pants, and each time I've wanted you. In fact,' he said, running an appreciative hand down the curves of her body, 'I wanted you the first time I saw you. I coveted you, Debbie. My brother's wife...of all people!' he mused in an undertone.

'Pia was his wife,' Debbie said hoarsely, her courage fading away with the shock of his caress.

'I don't regard her as such,' he replied softly, gazing into her eyes. 'She was more of a social asset. A decorative piece. Whereas I know that you would have tried your best to be a good wife to Gio. In every way.'

She tried to clear her throat and speak. To no avail.

'I find you entrancing,' he murmured. 'Make no mistake about it. If you stay, you must take the responsibility for encouraging me.' His eyes gleamed. 'I'm aroused every time I'm near you. I can't go on like that, can I? I'll be a nervous wreck,' he said disarmingly.

'This is part of your ploy to make me go! Ev-everyone can find self-control if they try,' she mumbled primly, wishing she could find a little more herself.

'Not always. Sometimes...' Luciano's sculptured mouth arched sensually '...sometimes our passionate natures rebel against being held under tight control. That's what has happened to me, to you.'

'No!' she cried sharply. 'Not me!'

There was an eloquent shrug of his shoulders and disbelief on his face. 'If you say so. But I am completely bewitched. I must have you—I will have you if you stay, because I won't be able to help myself.' He gave a slow, faintly menacing smile.

'I don't believe you! This is all about asserting power, isn't it?' she rasped, trying to wrench her hand from his and put some decent distance between them. 'You can't...you don't——'

'No?' He stood up quickly, their bodies swaying together. And before she could gather her wits he had placed her hand between them on the proof of his desire. 'A little crude in terms of proof,' he said thickly, his eyes lingering smokily on her parted lips and her huge, soft eyes. 'But how else could I convince you?'

'Please,' she begged in a hoarse whisper. 'Maria...Steffy...'

'I know,' he soothed, taking her in his arms. 'Public, isn't it?'

She wilted. The urge to lift her hands and curl them around the nape of his neck was almost too strong for her to deny. But she did and she pushed against the hard, muscular chest, a little appalled at the fierce heat that was passing between her loins and his.

Something practical came to her. 'I have to phone my mother,' she parried frantically.

'To tell her you'll be going home with Stefano after all?' he murmured, resting his hands seductively on her thigh and awakening a slow, delicious anticipation within her.

She almost said yes to free herself from his persistent attentions. Suddenly it dawned on her that he wanted a panic reaction. He wanted her to go so that he could take over the estate without delay. And he was working with every ounce of his will-power to make her leave, knowing that she'd be shocked by his proposition.

Sure, she wanted to leave, but she didn't want to be manipulated. The Colleoni brothers had done too much of that, she thought resentfully. Gio had coaxed and lied and cheated and she'd been fool enough to fall for every one of his silver-tongued declarations.

She flushed. One brother had made an idiot out of her. It wouldn't happen again.

'I'll be telling my mother that Steffy and I are both staying for a couple of days,' she told him defiantly. 'We'll be thinking things over.' And to hell with what he made of that! He wasn't going to force her to do anything she didn't want, and she'd make him sweat for a while.

'I'm not sure whether I'm pleased or sorry,' he said with an engagingly rueful grin. 'Every cloud has a silver lining, I suppose.'

'It'll rain blows on your head if you don't stop touching me,' she said grimly. Luciano laughed again, confounding her with his delight. 'The telephone,' she said tightly, horrified that part of her longed to say, Kiss me, instead, because his mouth looked so utterly kissable.

'Use that one,' he said in amusement, releasing her and indicating the hand-set by the window. His eyes crinkled. 'Then you won't have to worry about leaving your son alone with Maria and me.'

Haughtily, and hoping that her stiff manner would conceal the fact that her legs were wobbling all over the place, she went to the telephone and allowed Luciano to write down the code for her.

When she had finished the call and had replaced the receiver, she shot Luciano a puzzled look. 'My mother says there's twenty thousand pounds in our business account,' she said bluntly.

'Yes.'

'I thought it might be from you. What is it for?' she asked warily.

'Gio kept you short when he was alive,' Luciano replied quietly. 'It takes a man of great dishonour *not* to look after the mother of his child.' He met Debbie's pained eyes with some sympathy. 'I thought it only right that you should have something from his trust fund before Pia got her hands on it. I didn't know how to credit your personal account but my secretary had the number of your bank where you have your business account.'

His gesture astonished and embarrassed her. 'I couldn't . . .' she began huskily.

'You must. Unless you think you don't deserve a share of Gio's fortune?'

'I only wanted his love,' she told him stiffly.

'And you had to share even that——' his eyes glittered '—with the person Gio loved most.'

Miserable, she turned away. She knew who that was; the scales had fallen from her eyes. Gio had loved Gio. As for the money . . . Her shoulders drooped. 'What strings are attached to your generosity?' she asked suspiciously.

'None. It's a payment of honour.'

'Honour'. Bitterly she reflected that Luciano was the most unlikely man to be talking about honour—even Gio's mother thought so. And yet he had given her money when he didn't need to—unless, she thought in agitation, he intended to make that part of his pay-off.

Nothing was making sense. Only that she wanted to sleep and sleep and sleep. To forget everything and to be carefree again. 'I'm so tired,' she whispered flatly. 'So very tired.'

'It's not surprising. I'll carry Steffy up to your room for you,' Luciano said with surprising gentleness. 'He looks as if he'll be dead to the world for a while longer. You can lock yourself in and curl up with him for an hour or so. I imagine your luggage has arrived and you can settle yourself in.'

Her luggage! A picture of herself wearing the same clothes day in, day out came into her exhausted mind. 'I only have one change of clothes,' she said wearily.

'An old pair of jeans and a shirt I brought to wear home so that my cousin's suit won't get spoiled.'

Luciano's mouth tightened. 'Your cousin's suit?'

'Well, you don't think I'd intentionally buy one that was so ill-fitting, do you?' she snapped irritably. 'I had to borrow it. What the hell do you think I am?'

'Hard done by,' he growled. 'I think you and your mother deserve that money more than anyone I know. Take it. It should have been yours by rights.'

'Please,' she protested miserably, pushing her heavy hair back with a tired hand. 'I've had enough.'

'Perhaps if you rest your mind will be clearer. When you've thought things through, you'll be able to make the right decision.'

'I don't want to decide now,' she said fretfully.

'You must be feeling homesick,' he mused. 'I expect your mother is missing you.'

'Oh, don't,' she wailed. 'I'm shattered, Luciano...'

'I want you to be clear about a few things before you rest,' he said seriously, his voice oozing over her weary mind like smooth honey. 'While you're alone, you'll be able to turn over the pros and cons in your mind. I know you're wavering. Maybe you think it would be best if Stefano stayed here. But remember, your son would turn into a stranger. His life would be far removed from what you know—your own culture, your environment, your language. He wouldn't be your son at all, would he? Stefano would be the heir of a great estate, one which has been in the Colleoni family for hundreds of years, the stamping-ground of generations of noblemen. And he'd become one too.'

'Don't you think I know that?' she muttered unhappily.

'But do you understand what it means in reality?' Luciano asked softly. 'Even if you stayed here with him he would become a Sicilian male. He would have to, to take his place in society. Could you bear to see your son become more and more estranged from you every day? You are blunt and firm and down-to-earth in your methods of child-rearing in England. Could you watch him taking on the arrogance that comes from the un-stinting adoration showered on a male child in this country?'

'N-no, but I'd make sure——'

He shook his head. 'No, Debbie. Whether you stayed or not, you'd be one lone voice in a sea of Sicilian tra-dition and you'd be helpless. He'd see how his friends were treated, the liberties they'd be allowed. He'd hate you for restricting him, for denying him whatever he wanted, and he'd resent your discipline. Naturally, he would increasingly avoid you and spend his time with the women of the family who would indulge him.'

With a frank, concerned expression in his dark eyes, he placed his hands on her shoulders and she felt so bur-dened that she thought she might sink with the weight of responsibility. 'I want you to consider this when you're alone in your room,' Luciano said gravely. 'Let's not beat about the bush. You'd lose your son. Could you really give him up? Don't you love him?'

'Of course I do!' she cried piteously. 'Stop spelling out all the things I know already. You're being unfair.'

Taking her face in his hands, he looked down on her with his liquid dark eyes and said earnestly, 'I'm making sure you know the consequences of any decision you come to. I urge you to leave, whether tonight or in a few days, and to take your son with you.'

'You—you said you wanted to make love to me. Oh, this is difficult!' she said, blushing furiously. 'Yet you're telling me to go...'

'I want you,' he uttered. 'But I want something else more.'

'The house. The land,' she said in a low voice.

He seemed to be struggling with his emotions. 'Believe that if you want to,' he growled. 'But, whatever you do, pretend that the Colleoni don't even exist. Your mother doesn't know. Stefano need never know. He'll be told good things about his father and you'll be well off and able to lead a comfortable life. Isn't that tempting? He would be your son for the rest of his life, Debbie,' he said passionately. 'Go home and keep your son. You wouldn't lose him as you might here.'

Trembling, she swayed with exhaustion and Luciano gathered her close. He was warm and she was cold. He offered a shoulder to lean on and she needed one, so she clung to him gratefully. But although he seemed sincere and caring she knew he couldn't have her interests at heart. Only his own.

So like Gio.

With a sudden movement, she pushed herself away—away from the false security that Luciano was offering. She had to stand alone. A decision must be made, but she must make it in her own time and not because some smooth-talking guy had coaxed her into believing what he wanted her to believe.

'I want to rest,' she whispered harshly, appalled at the choices she faced. 'Show me where.'

A glitter of disappointment slashed the warm blackness of his eyes like the glint of a sword. 'I'll carry Stefano up,' he growled and she was too bone-weary to protest.

After sleeping, she felt better. The shuttered room was dark and cool and she'd slept as soundly as Steffy, even though she'd expected to lie awake fretting over her worries. But she must have been more tired than she'd imagined because she had fallen asleep almost as soon as her head hit the pillow.

When she woke, she wandered in her underwear over to the window, opened the shutters again and leaned out, looking at the cloistered garden. The silence astonished her. She'd never been far from the sound of traffic before and the utter stillness and lush greenery beckoned to her enticingly. Maybe, she mused, if she could sit there for a while, she might get a better perspective on things.

With dubious eyes, she contemplated the black suit which she had carefully hung up in the wardrobe. Somehow she didn't care to wear it, and she had no intention of digging into her thoughts and examining why that should be. She had enough to worry about. So, she'd wear the jeans.

Her hands drew them from the small overnight bag and she wriggled into them, fastening the stud across her flat stomach. Her fingers stilled. In a sudden flash of awareness, she glanced up at her reflection to see what Luciano would see if he ever tried to carry out his threat to coax her into bed.

The first thing she noticed was that her grey eyes seemed as dark as charcoal and were shining feverishly. Wonderingly, she touched the soft waves of her hair, startlingly blonde in the bright rays of sunshine that came through the open window. And her breasts...

She frowned and peered harder. Had they always been *quite* as voluptuous? Perhaps she'd been innocently giving out sexual messages, and Luciano had read them and made his own interpretation. Hurriedly she put on the shirt, firmly buttoned it up to hide the evidence from view and tiptoed over to Stefano. He was still asleep. He'd have to come with her.

She carried him carefully down the stairs, and placed him on a blanket in a shady and secluded corner of the garden beneath the drooping racemes of an enormous, gnarled wisteria.

The whole house seemed to be sleeping, the shuttered rooms like closed eyes. It was a rare, stolen moment of peace and solitude and she sat on a low wall, listening

to the Mediterranean sounds of the afternoon and inhaling the heady scent of the roses.

What a house. And it could be Steffy's. It didn't
matter what was best for her; she had to decide what
would be best for him. In the material sense, there was
no question. Even taking into account Luciano's generous financial offer, Steffy would be better off here,
installed as his father's heir. He'd have a wonderful life,
everything anyone could wish for and more. But
emotionally...

Her fingers idly traced a pattern on the lichen-covered
wall as she tried to work out what she'd do if Luciano
weren't around. She'd bring Steffy up here, probably,
and ask her mother to live with her and help to stop
Steffy becoming spoilt. Of course they'd take on board
the way children were brought up in Sicily, but somehow
they'd get a good balance between them.

Unfortunately, Luciano was all too present. And he
found her attractive. Even though he was using his
sexuality as a weapon to frighten her, he *had* been
aroused, and living in Sicily would mean a constant battle
to keep him out of her bed. One day, given his persistence, given the way her hormones sprang into life
whenever he was around, she knew she would be sure
to weaken—and then where would that leave her?
Another Colleoni mistress, that was where!

Stefano would regard her with contempt. So would
the staff and the villagers. So would she.

In the meantime, her son would be inculcated with
the arts of being a Sicilian gentleman and she didn't like
the sound of what that meant.

Debbie clasped her hands in front of her tightly, her
eyes glazing over as her heart cramped at the thought
that she might be pushed aside. He was her child.
Although her mother had always been there if needed,
it was she, Debbie, who'd brought him up virtually

single-handed, struggling through sleepless nights, the teething problems, the never-ending worry about money that she'd kept from her mother...

Tears pricked her soulful grey eyes. She loved Stefano. He had become the centre of her life. Without him, she didn't know how she would exist. Her love for him was all-consuming; it made her heart go tight when she thought of him. He gave her joy and a feeling of intense passion that words couldn't express.

No. She couldn't give him up to the Colleoni family. And even now she wondered if she was wise to stay for the night. Luciano might seem civilised on the surface, but he was a ruthless, embittered man who had given every indication of plotting some vicious and mal-evolent fate for the little boy who stood in the way of the house and land he'd coveted for so long.

She stared at the flowerbed and sighed because she knew that she was back to her original state of wavering indecision again.

Slowly her eyes focused on a weed and without thinking she knelt on the grass and pulled it out. Then another. And soon she had worked her way along the bed, finding it therapeutic not to think for a while. Perhaps the solution to her problem would come of its own accord. It did that sometimes.

'*Ciao*!' sang out a cheery voice.

Debbie looked up, startled, and shaded her eyes. A rather grubby-looking woman, about her own age, was coming up the path with a pair of secateurs in her hand.

'Um...*ciao*,' Debbie said uncertainly.

'Gawd! End of conversation!' the woman said to herself, planting her filthy hands in the pockets of her ancient, cut-off shorts. 'That's the only Italian I know.'

'It's about all I know too.' Debbie found herself smiling a little.

'Well, I'm blowed!' grinned the woman in astonishment. 'I'm Sue. I'm from Lambeth.'

'Oh, not far from me! I live in Southwark. I'm Debbie.' And she thought what a relief it was, meeting someone sane and homely for a change.

'Thought so. What a turn-up.' Sue nodded towards the pile of weeds. 'You're doing a good job there. Everything grows like the clappers and the weeds are getting on top of me. Luciano said he'd get more gardeners, bless his heart, but I never thought he'd do it so fast. Bit like everything else he does, I suppose. What a sweetie he is.'

Debbie blinked at Sue's smiling endearments. 'He is?' she said faintly. 'What do you mean, "like everything else he does"?'

'Oh, word is that he took over some bank,' said Sue breezily. 'Whipped in there like a ferret after a rabbit, sacked a whole layer of management and left everyone trembling. *Then*, in the middle of all of that, he comes here when his brother dies, hurls questions at everyone, and bingo! The kitchen's being done because he's appalled that Maria and co have to work in such terrible conditions, and we're getting new staff quarters—and more pay.' Sue cocked her head on one side engagingly. 'Can't be bad, can it?'

'No. Sounds...very dynamic,' said Debbie cautiously.

'Actually, I was on the point of handing in my notice when Luciano breezed in. You're lucky you've come to work for him and not his little brute of a brother.'

Debbie's hand faltered. 'Mmm,' she muttered noncommittally, hiding her flaming face in some soft-leaved plant with spiky blue flowers.

'Well, Gio was a right little lecher, I can tell you,' confided Sue. 'Ask any of the girls who work here. I only had to bend down and the little rat was pinching my bottom. And whenever I turned round to thump him he'd try to grab me you-know-where.'

'Oh!' It was all Debbie could manage. Somewhere inside her she was choking with misery.

'Course,' went on Sue blithely, scowling at a dandelion, 'Gio's family were totally hoodwinked by him. They thought the sun shone out of his you-know-what. Smarmy little devil!' she said viciously, then caught Debbie's look. 'Yeah, I know. But call a spade a spade, I reckon, and if I'd only paid attention at school and learnt a few more words I'd fling them around too. I can't tell you how much he harassed the female staff.'

'They could have left,' suggested Debbie hoarsely, and cleared her throat of the huge lump there.

'Difficult. When you're hard up you gotta take any work you can, haven't you?'

Debbie nodded, her mind going over and over what Sue had said. It was true, she was sure. Sue didn't seem the sort to tell tales and her indignation was genuine enough. She'd half known the sort of man Gio was, but it wasn't nice to have her suspicions confirmed.

'What about Luciano?' she asked hoarsely. 'Isn't he a bit like that too?'

'You want to look after that cold,' said Sue sympathetically. 'Ask Maria for some garlic and lemon and honey. Smashing! Luciano sent me off for a dose of that the first day he came and it did the trick. Nice of him to notice, when he was juggling a million things in the air at once. Flaming marvellous, he is. Straight, you know what I mean? If he doesn't like something, he says so. I like to know where I am. We've all decided he's a million per cent improvement on his horrible brother.'

'Luciano,' Debbie said shakily. 'He seems very... sexual.'

'Do me a favour!' scoffed Sue. 'Not a hint of it. Wishful thinking on your part, I reckon. He's got this secretary who's been with him for ten years and she says he's got strict principles about how he treats his staff— and sex is taboo. Some of us'd welcome a bit of a flirt with him,' she sighed. 'Lovely hunk. Got a lovely smile.'

Thoroughly muddled and deeply embarrassed by the revelations, Debbie kept quiet while Sue chattered away, extolling Luciano's virtues. And there were plenty. It was almost as if they knew two different men.

But she remembered the old lady on the crossing who'd dropped her shopping, his concerned telephone calls after Gio's death, his unprompted gift of money to her business account. It was possible that Luciano was the saint his staff seemed intent on idolising. In which case, she argued, why was he being so foul to *her*? Whatever Sue said, he was trying to compromise her sexually for his own ends. He was unprincipled, she thought bitterly, her mouth drooping at the corners.

Deep down, she knew that there was more to it than met the eye. Luciano was clever. He had some other reason for his actions and if she could only work out what it was she might be able to gain control of the situation.

Sue's easy chatter drifted on in the background as Debbie became immersed in her own private thoughts. She didn't hear the footsteps on the gravel till Sue called, 'Hey, Luciano! *Ciao*!'

'Oh, hell,' muttered Debbie crossly. Now Sue would discover who she was.

'Hi.' Sue jumped up and stood looking at Luciano in frank admiration while Debbie did her best to hide her scarlet face in another clump of the blue stuff. 'Thanks for finding Debbie,' Sue enthused happily. 'We're getting on like a house on fire. It's great to have a fellow gardener from south of the river.'

'Ah, yes, I suppose it is,' came Luciano's amused voice. 'Looks a bit red in the face, don't you think?'

'Sun. Not used to it. Hey, Debs, why don't you stop for a bit? We can take a break now and go and get a drink and sit in the shade for a while.'

'No, I—I...'

'You go, Sue,' said Luciano smoothly. 'There are a couple of documents Debbie needs to sign. Come into my study,' he ordered abruptly in a soft but don't-defy-me voice.

Her eyes darted to where Steffy lay close by. 'I think I ought to finish weeding this bed,' she began uncomfortably. A small cry betrayed why she couldn't leave. Steffy rolled over grumpily and sat up, rubbing his eyes.

'Oh, look at the dear little scrap,' cooed Sue. 'Is he yours, Debs? Hey, Luciano, can I take him to see the ducks in my breaktime? Like to see the ducks?' she asked the blinking Stefano.

He nodded and scrambled to his feet. He and Debbie had spent many a lonely Sunday feeding ducks in the park. 'Ducks, please!' he said eagerly, turning the full power of his dark eyes on Sue.

'What a good idea. If you would entertain...Steffy... for a while,' said Luciano blandly, 'Debbie can get the papers signed. Take an hour or so off. We'll come and find you.'

Debbie groaned. 'No,' she said firmly.

'Steffy will be all right with Sue,' said Luciano gently. 'You can trust her.' He lifted a sardonic eyebrow. 'I'm sure you won't want me to bring the documents out here and discuss your situation while you work. It would be *so* uncomfortable.'

It was a loaded threat. He could see that she didn't want Sue to know who she was. She flushed scarlet in shame.

'Course she can trust me,' grinned Sue as Steffy impatiently hopped up and down, waiting for her to show him the ducks. 'Okey-dokey?'

'Okey-dokey,' said Debbie faintly. 'Steffy, be good. Stay with Sue and don't go with anyone else.'

'Okey-dokey,' grinned Stefano.

Debbie watched him toddle away with mixed feelings. Gio's son. God! she thought, shivering with a sudden icy chill as Sue's revelations began to sink in. She prayed that Stefano would never treat a woman with the same contempt that his father had. Her lower lip quivered. She didn't want to think about it. The whole thing was so sordid.

'What's wrong?' asked Luciano with quiet concern, tipping up her chin.

Too distressed to share her feelings, she jerked away, but he persisted, his palm drawing her face back till she had to look at him, all the misery of the last few minutes clear in her moist eyes. 'I—I . . .' To her horror, the tears began to fall. Hot, salty, torrents of tears.

'Come,' said Luciano gently.

And, being blind, she had to let him lead her to goodness knew where. Up steps, along a corridor, and then she was in a room, its blaze of light muted as he closed the shutters. His arm came firmly around her waist and she was drawn down to a sofa. The arm stayed in place.

Rubbing her eyes with a handkerchief, she saw from the book-lined walls and the large desk that they must be in his study. 'Leave me,' she said, her voice muffled by tears.

'No, you need to talk. You've had a few shocks in the last few days. I think we have to——'

'I don't want to talk to you,' she said obstinately. 'It's been *foul* today. I want to end it. I've had enough. I never thought that Gio. . .' Aghast, she clamped her mouth shut. But Luciano had taken her arms and was giving her a little shake. 'I won't talk about it,' she wailed. 'I won't.'

'Did Sue tell you about him?' Luciano asked sharply. Debbie nodded, too miserable to say anything. 'Damn! What?' he demanded.

She remained mute, her eyelashes fluttering as the tears welled up and spilled on to her cheeks.

'I'll have to go and ask her,' he said curtly.

'No!' she cried, her glance flashing up in alarm. 'No, Luciano, please! I couldn't bear it. I—I can't get used to the fact that I was never properly married. I hate people knowing. And I like Sue. I don't want her to think badly of me.'

'She wouldn't,' growled Luciano. 'Only of my brother. It would confirm what she already thinks of him.'

'He was...' She swallowed. 'He was a swine, wasn't he?'

'Tell me what you know.'

She did so. And knew that his anger wasn't directed at her but at his brother as he watched her face and saw how much it hurt her to speak of Gio's failings. He coaxed her to talk about Gio's behaviour at home and he became very quiet and unnaturally still, his mouth taking on a thin line and his eyes becoming narrower and narrower as she poured out her heart in a stumbling, faltering voice.

'I'm sorry,' he said huskily when she'd finished. 'You've had a rotten time.'

She shrugged. 'I was busy working to survive,' she explained. 'When you're on the breadline, all your energies are concentrated on keeping yourself, day by day. You don't have time to think much, or to ponder the future. I got on with day-to-day living.'

'You're brave and tough and I admire you very much.'

Luciano's warm compliments touched her heart. 'Thank you,' she breathed shakily.

'You still have a great deal: your mother, a loving family, Stefano,' he murmured quietly in the semi-darkness. 'That's more than most people. You're fortunate. You've lost a great deal, I'm not denying that, but you have something very special, Debbie. Cherish it, nurture it, be glad.'

'You're right,' she said tremulously. 'And I'll be all right in a moment. It was just so awful, hearing such a damning, uncensored opinion of Gio. I can't stop trembling,' she complained, annoyed with herself for being so pathetic.

'I'll hold you,' he offered huskily. 'Till you feel stronger.'

They sat in the half-light for some time. Debbie felt numb and lifeless. Luciano was right. In fact, she hadn't lost anything, because the true love of a faithful husband had never been in her possession. And she'd gained knowledge, caution and perhaps a greater appreciation of her family and their love and caring concern.

'I want Stefano to be the centre of love,' she said quietly. 'I want him to grow up knowing what's right and what's wrong, to have decent values and never to hurt people weaker or unluckier than him. I want him to be content with what he has and not to envy others. And I want to be there, guiding him, helping him to find how to be comfortable with himself.'

'Then...' Luciano's voice was rough, as if emotion choked his throat. When she looked up she saw that his face was suddenly bleak, the skin stretched taut across his high cheekbones. 'Then,' he repeated almost inaudibly, as if it was an effort to speak, 'you know you have to take him home.'

'Yes.' She met his eyes. A pain, as sharp as a knife, shot through her body and she gasped aloud in shock.

'Debbie,' he husked. He bent his head, his intention clear. He was going to kiss her. And she wanted him to with a force so strong that it terrified her. But he suddenly rose with an abrupt movement and turned to his desk. 'I'll get you on the first flight out of here,' he rasped.

The sense of disappointment overwhelmed her. Appalled, she pinned her gaze to his broad back as if wishing could make him turn back to her, kiss her, tell her that...

She dug her teeth into her lower lip. Foolish thoughts. But she couldn't take her eyes off him as he shuffled papers and thumbed through a notebook. 'I—I won't see you again after today, then,' she said unhappily.

'No.' The notebook slipped from his fingers and he cursed, then retrieved it, absorbed in searching for something. Debbie was upset that his manner was stiff and his tone had been curt. 'I don't think we need bother one another again.' She strained to hear his muffled words. 'It wouldn't be wise, would it? When you leave, we'll make our final goodbyes.'

'Final goodbyes.' She sank limply back, her lips parted in dismay. She'd never see him again. And in a blinding flash she knew with a painful poignancy that Luciano could have made her happy. In time she would have fallen in love with him—if she hadn't done so already.

She knew that because her heart felt sick. The life force inside her was dying, second by second, at the depressing promise of a future without him. She'd fallen for him hook, line and sinker. And she was deliberately walking out of his life of her own free will.

CHAPTER EIGHT

LUCIANO dialled a number, presumably the airline's. Debbie walked out of the room, somehow making her legs move despite their reluctance to do so.

At the top of the sweep of stairs she paused because her body had resisted every step she'd taken away from him. From the full-length window she watched Steffy's tiny figure happily running around the lake with Sue. With a weariness beyond exhaustion, she reflected sentimentally that her son would never know that this had been his house. He'd never know the love of a father with Luciano's strong qualities—his immense vigour, his passion, his compassion.

And more. So much more. Luciano was so complex that she doubted she had learnt everything about him. Yet she knew instinctively that he would run this estate and all his other enterprises fairly. He'd already earned the respect of the staff here. Better that she should go, before Luciano spoiled her good opinion of him by attempting to lure her into bed.

She must pack. Collect Steffy.

She gripped the tiled ledge of the window, her lethargy turning to misery. She didn't want to leave. The thought of going away left her with a sense of bereavement which was so intense and sharp that she winced from it. Luciano had invaded her heart and her soul, deeply, irrevocably.

'Debbie.'

She jumped, her nerves skittering everywhere. Luciano's footsteps were coming across the hallway.

163

They stopped at the foot of the stairs and she waited listlessly, without turning, to hear the time of her flight.

When he didn't speak, she slowly turned, her whole body heavy and solid with the burden of her secret love. He was looking up at her with an inscrutable expression on his face and she wanted to run down the stairs and throw herself into his arms, to beg to be given a room somewhere so that she could be near him.

'For God's sake, Luciano,' she said hoarsely, appalled by her hopeless desires, 'tell me when I'm to go.'

'You're on edge,' he observed quietly, his eyes piercing.

'No, I'm not!' she yelled.

'You're upset about Gio?' he asked carefully.

'No,' she moaned. 'Yes . . . Oh, Luciano, I have to tell you before I . . . before I go. I can't leave you with—without telling you. I don't know now if I ever loved Gio; I was charmed by him and I kept our marriage going for Stefano's sake.' She tried to stop her voice from wobbling. 'My feelings for him died long ago. I'm not sure . . . I'm not sure I ever liked him. There. Now you'll think I'm a fool . . .'

A long breath rasped from his lungs. 'On the contrary,' he said softly. 'I think you're wise and loyal and I admire you for trying your best. And for being such a good mother to Stefano.'

She let out a sob. It would have been easier to say farewell if he'd been unkind and contemptuous. This gentle flattery was hard to bear. 'Oh, Luciano,' she said, the words jumping up and down the scales. 'You've got the flight? When? When is it to be?' she cried, wringing her hands.

His velvet eyes regarded her without blinking but she sensed that he was calm and infinitely at ease with himself, a fact that distressed her when she was in such torment.

'I didn't get a flight,' he said levelly, 'so you can go back on the one you booked for tomorrow.'

She half fell with a joyous relief and clutched at the ledge again, her legs shaking uncontrollably. 'Tomorrow? Oh, tomorrow,' she repeated stupidly. 'That's...'

It was wonderful. And she turned away because the thought of a few more hours with Luciano was both a pain and a delight. The hammering of her heart obliterated everything in her mind. Time with Luciano, and then...the anguish of parting. Her eyes clouded. She would still have to leave him. And her love would be even stronger tomorrow.

'Is that a problem?' he asked, a smile in his voice.

'Yes! No... Perhaps I'd better get a taxi,' she rasped. 'Now,' she added, half hysterical with the need to get away before she betrayed her feelings. 'Steffy and I can go to Palermo and wait there.'

'But you won't get a flight till tomorrow. What's the point? You'd have to pay exorbitant prices for a place to stay,' he argued. 'You might as well remain here, where it's free.'

'Free'. If only she could be free. Tension stretched every nerve in her body. There would be the night to get through. Maybe Luciano would try to seduce her. And she'd have to stop him.

'I know how upset you are. I'll keep out of your way,' he said quietly.

'No—!' Appalled, she blinked. How had that come out? 'I mean...yes. Yes, thank you,' she said chokingly. He must know, she thought. He must see how passionately she wanted to stay.

Apparently not. 'Make yourself at home. We eat at eight in the main dining-room. Ask anyone where that is. I'll leave you now.'

She heard his footsteps receding and waited till he'd gone. Then she stumbled down the stairs, knowing that even her darling Steffy couldn't heal the misery in her heart.

Sue didn't question her glum face. The two of them worked in the garden and supervised Steffy. Hard work relieved some of Debbie's anguish, but not the sense of despair.

She'd never felt so gloomy before. The prospect of leaving Luciano appalled her. It was as if she'd never be happy again and she found it astonishing that she felt so dependent on another human being for happiness.

Now she really understood what her mother had gone through when her father had died. At sixteen, she'd been old enough to know how much her parents had loved one another—and her own love for her father had made her grieve deeply—but now she imagined she knew what the real loss of a loving partner meant. A partner was part of you and when he or she went part of you died too.

Part of her was dying. She was already in mourning and would go on mourning for the rest of her life because she knew with absolute certainty that Luciano was the man for her and that there would never be another like him. She was throwing away her future happiness. She wanted to stay. Oh, yes, she wanted to stay!

Her desolate eyes lifted and she watched Steffy, contentedly sorting the gravel into little heaps, and poignant pain slashed through her body with the force of a butcher's knife, making her cry out loud.

'Debbie!' cried Sue, startled. She ran over and bent down where Debbie crouched, rocking in agony. 'What is it? What's happened?'

'Cramp,' she lied, grinding the word out through her teeth.

'You poor love, it's made you cry. How awful. Stand up. Waggle it about, whatever it is. I'll get Maria to do you one of her herbal thingummies.'

They both looked up to see Luciano racing out from the shadow of the cloister. 'What's the matter, Debbie?' he called urgently.

'She's got cramp,' Sue said.

'I'll take her in.'

'No,' Debbie protested as Luciano advanced. He couldn't touch her. If he did . . . 'Oh, for heaven's sake!' she snapped, when he picked her up like a child. 'Steffy——'

'Bring him, Sue,' ordered Luciano abruptly, his eyes far too piercing for Debbie's comfort. 'To the study. Then go to Maria for some *arnica montana*.'

'I know. Herby stuff. I've had it. Okey-dokey,' said Sue good-humouredly.

'Set me down,' muttered Debbie as he purposefully strode off with her.

'No,' he said firmly.

'Set me *down*,' she grated in panic.

'I think you're ill.' He frowned. 'Maybe it's more than cramp. Your face is flushed, your eyes are bright, your hands are clammy——'

'I'm all right. It's—it's the heat. Don't you understand?' she whispered, hoping that Sue's chattering as she jollied Steffy along would hide what she was saying. 'I don't want to be touched by you.'

'Really? Have you always been stubborn?' he murmured.

'I can be worse than this,' she returned jerkily. Luciano's face was so close that her breath rebounded from his smooth golden skin—and it was making him flinch, which was odd. Faster and shallower, her breath fanned his skin and she felt his own quicken in his powerful chest.

Of course. He was carrying her and he had become aroused again. 'Don't leave me, Sue,' she croaked when they reached the study.

'Don't be daft!' Sue grinned. 'Luciano's with you. And you're not likely to die of cramp.'

Debbie stared at the closing door in alarm and then up at Luciano, her eyes softening and growing wider and wider as her heart leapt about madly. How *stupid* she was! She felt she might die of longing.

'You'll sit there and wait for Maria to bring you something that will ease your muscles from the work,' he said sternly, placing her with heart-wrenching gentleness on a *chaise-longue*.

'I'm used to hard work,' she muttered.

'I know, but your body has been drained by shock,' he soothed. 'You need to give it time to recover.'

'I wanted to do something physical,' she grumbled.

He smiled as if that made him happy. 'Yes, I know. I do understand. But rest now. I will continue to work. Enrico will bring Steffy some of his children's toys and you will stay here till it's time to freshen up for dinner.' His eyes glimmered. 'I think I know what's wrong with you, but I want to keep an eye on you for a while.' He positively grinned. 'Just to make sure.'

'It's not necessary,' she insisted, from the depths of the soft cushions.

'It is. Damn well do as you're told for a change!'

She subsided. It was pleasant to be waited on. People came and went, offering her herbal drinks, magazines, and dainty sandwiches which she couldn't eat. Luciano abandoned any attempt to work and returned to play with Steffy, helping him to build simple brick walls for half a dozen toy cars.

And the two of them contentedly drove the cars around the legs of the furniture and into the tunnels Luciano had carefully constructed from sheets of card and sticky tape, with Steffy excitedly calling his attention to something he'd done with a 'Look, Sarno! Sarno, look!' that half broke her heart.

Every now and then Luciano would look up at her and her breath would catch in her throat. The tone of his voice when he asked how she was feeling made her heart lurch in anguish. She wanted him to care, really care. Not because she might be feeling ill, but because he loved her.

And poignant again was the experience of watching Luciano playing so sweetly and lovingly with her son as if he were Steffy's father, and knowing that tomorrow they would all be saying goodbye. Her mind and her heart dreamed. And the pain tormented her with the knowledge that this was a relationship that could never be.

The dining-room was lit by the golden glow of soft candlelight. Debbie hesitated in the doorway, conscious of the fact that her shirt and jeans didn't really complement the exuberant richness of the lovely damasks and tapestries of the room.

Rising from his seat at the head of the vast, gleaming table, Luciano beckoned her over. 'Come in. Sit by me. How are you now?' he asked warmly.

'All right,' she mumbled, stunned by his handsome looks.

Tonight he was every inch the new gentleman owner of the Villa di Leoni in his superbly tailored dinner-jacket—tall, dark, elegant. She wanted to touch his newly shaven cheek, to kiss the dark-lidded eyes and let her tongue shape the finely chiselled mouth. Instead, she walked stiffly to the seat on his right and sat down.

Unfairly, he spread a napkin on her lap, his fingers briefly touching her thighs. And through the thickness of her cheap jeans she felt the burning fire that characterised his every caress, however unintentional it might be.

'Maria has produced some specialities to tempt your appetite,' he said softly. 'Shall we kick off with some champagne?'

Her hurt eyes met his. What was there to celebrate? She caught a gleam of satisfaction in his gaze and realised that for him this was a celebration. He was the undisputed master here at last; his ambitions had been fulfilled.

'No—thanks,' she jerked out miserably.

Unaware of her distress, he made small talk and she tried to reply but the words were choking her and she wished she were upstairs, like Steffy, fast asleep and ignorant of the pains of a one-sided love.

'You're not eating,' he observed quietly after a while.

'I can't,' she mumbled. 'I've tried. I don't want to upset Maria . . . I've pushed the food around so she's not offended. I—I'm not hungry.'

'I see.' There was a faint smile playing around his mouth and she pouted in resentment. Judging by the suppressed excitement in every move of his body, he was overjoyed with life. She felt utterly depressed. He reached over and removed the untouched chicken dish in front of her. 'You won't want pudding, then, I take it?' he asked, all innocence.

'No.'

'You're not happy, are you?' he murmured, his mouth twitching.

'Why shouldn't I be?' she snapped with something of her old spirit.

'No reason,' he said, and brought up his hand as if to hide a smile.

'I'm going home. I love my home,' she went on doggedly, wondering why she sounded as if she was diving into lumpy porridge. 'I love my mother. I want to be home. I want to be with my mother.'

'And you'll have fifty thousand a year. You'll have a wonderful life,' said Luciano brightly.

'Oh—that.' It was a fortune. It would give her everything she and her mother had dreamed of and offer Steffy a great start. And it wasn't enough. Yet people she knew—including her, once—would have given their right arm for that kind of security.

'You don't sound very enthusiastic,' he chided gently.

Glumly she picked at the stitching on the mane of the lion which had been embroidered with loving care on the damask tablecloth. 'It's incredibly generous,' she said dutifully. 'Half that would be more than generous.'

'Good. Well, would you like to go into the drawing-room and have a last chat? Final gossip? Farewell natter? I imagine this'll be the last opportunity we'll have——'

'*No*,' she wailed.

'Oh,' he said politely as if it didn't surprise him in the least. He stretched luxuriously. 'In that case, we might as well turn in.'

Her head jerked around to him. He looked vastly amused and she drew in a wary breath. 'I hope you're not suggesting...?'

'Sex?' he murmured and she flushed. 'I don't think I need to threaten you, now you've decided categorically that you want to leave.'

'No,' she said, her mouth a thin, bitter line. 'You have what you want.'

'Almost,' he agreed, lowering his lashes.

Her mouth grew sulky. 'You have the villa and the land.'

'It should have been mine,' he said quietly. 'My father wanted me to have it.'

'But he must have known you couldn't.' Her brow furrowed. 'Gio was his elder son.'

'Not his favourite, though.' Luciano's long fingers traced the lion crest on the champagne flute in front of him. He gave her a gentle smile. 'I'd like to tell you about my father. Can I? I want you to understand about him, you see,' he said earnestly. 'I don't want you to think badly of him.'

How could she refuse him anything, even when it meant sitting there and biting her lip to stop herself from reaching out and smoothing away his anxious frown?

'I'd like to hear,' she said weakly. Anything to watch him talking, to postpone the moment when they must part. She'd talk to him all night if she could.

'I want you to know that Father wasn't an immoral man. He told me when he was dying that he'd tried to make a go of his marriage.' Luciano sighed. 'But when Gio was born Father became an outcast in his own house. Everything centred on Gio: Gio this, Gio that. He felt unloved and lonely.'

'So he took a mistress,' she said, unable to keep the disapproval from her voice.

'It's not that simple,' Luciano replied huskily, turning his gaze on her, his smouldering eyes aflame from the candlelight. 'Life never is. Father threw himself into work. And he fell hopelessly, irrevocably in love with his secretary. For the rest of his life—for nearly twenty years—they remained in love, faithful to one another, caring for one another, in sickness and in health, as if they were truly married.

'Father was discreet,' he continued softly. 'Never once did he allow it to be generally known that he loved another woman. Finola—my mother—lived on the Lipari Islands and he always used a very tortuous route to get there.'

Debbie tried to work out how she felt about that. Marriage was marriage. And yet...she saw Luciano's passion as he described his father's love for Finola. Knowing how she felt about him, she was beginning to realise what love could do to someone.

'I could never be unfaithful to my lawful husband,' she said.

'Nor I to my wife.' Luciano hesitated and then touched her hand with the lightest of gestures. 'But then, Debbie, I would never marry unless I knew without a shadow of doubt that I was marrying the woman I could love till my dying day. I've seen what infidelity can do. I have no wish to marry without being struck by that violent bolt of lightning called love.'

Wryly she wished it would hurtle out of the sky *now* and strike him where he sat. 'Your father brought you to live here,' she remembered, her eyes shimmering with gentle love for him. 'How could your own mother have let you go?'

'Perhaps because she loved my father so much that she wanted him to have me near,' Luciano said with a smile. 'She knew he couldn't leave his wife and she was glad that she had Father's love—and mine.

'Besides,' he went on, 'I didn't come here straight away. I was nine on my first visit. You see, Father said I was a Colleoni, with Colleoni blood, and that I should know my heritage. He was already alarmed at the way Gio was being doted on. Gio ran riot around the house and behaved as he pleased. I won't tell you some of the things he did, but he had a streak of cruelty towards animals that sickened Father.'

'Didn't his mother discipline him at all?' she asked unhappily.

He shrugged. 'Gio could twist his mother around his little finger—and the rest of the family. And, as Gio grew up, I stayed longer on my visits and divided my time between my mother and my father.'

'Gio's mother must have hated you,' Debbie said soberly. 'It must have hurt her to have her husband's illegitimate child in the house.'

'Yes,' he acknowledged. 'At that time, however, I was too young and insensitive to care about her feelings because she was so cruel to me. I think Father badly needed me around to make his life more bearable, because for the sake of family honour he had to give the appearance of a happy marriage.'

'People must have known who—what—you were.'

'The family did, of course. But I went under my natural mother's name till Father officially adopted me. Everyone just thought he was fond of me and liked my company.'

Luciano took her hand in his and began to stroke it absently. 'My father was adamant that I should learn about the running of the estate and how to organise and motivate staff. He knew that when he died I'd be on my own and I'd need a range of skills at my disposal. And I loved it here, so I put up with the taunts, the ridicule, the physical bullying. I stuck it out for Father's sake—particularly in the last year of his life. My mother, Finola, had died that year, you see. He needed me.'

'And when he died?' she asked tentatively.

His mouth thinned. 'I was physically ejected on to the drive,' he answered.

'Oh, how *awful*! I can't bear to think——' She stopped in confusion, but squeezed his hand in sympathy.

'Thanks for your concern.' He looked deeply into her eyes. 'Gio's mother got her revenge,' he went on with a quiet sadness. 'She refused me permission to attend Father's funeral—as I was refused permission to be at Gio's graveside. But as my father had lain dying in my arms I had made a promise that I would watch out for the villa and not allow Gio to harm it. I think Father imagined that Gio would ruin himself one day, with drink or at the hand of a jealous husband or by reckless driving.'

'I see,' she said, thinking that Gio had taken many risks with his life and, in the end, had taken one too many.

'I'm sorry for what Gio's mother had to put up with,' mused Luciano, 'but she shouldn't have taken out her anger on me. I was an innocent child. I'm afraid she spread rumours about me in the village and turned the rest of the family against me. Not surprising, really. I really had a bad time at their hands, but it toughened me.' He gave a huge sigh. 'I only wish they and Gio hadn't been draining the estate dry.'

'Your father wanted you to live here,' she said gently. 'He—he has his wish now.' Even though, she thought, it was at the expense of her happiness.

'And I——' Luciano smiled contentedly, squeezing her hand in delight '—I am sure I have everything I could possibly want.'

She gave a choking cry and pretended something had gone down the wrong way, gulping down some of his offered champagne. Miserably, she reflected that she didn't have what she wanted: Luciano.

Before she completely broke down and howled like a deprived child, she had to get to her room. She stood up shakily and passed a hand across her moist eyes. 'Tired,' she muttered. 'Dog-tired.'

'Of course. Shall I see you up? No? Very well. You know the way,' he said placidly. 'Goodnight, then.'

For a moment she remained standing there, stunned by the callous simplicity of it all. A cool goodnight. Then she'd sleep and then she'd wake and then he'd get her on a flight and she'd leave. Finish. *Finito*. The end. But what did he care?

'Luciano...'

'Yes?' he said encouragingly.

She couldn't put herself on the line, couldn't tell him of her feelings. She felt too vulnerable. A shuddering breath rocketed through her body. 'Night!' she flung at him jerkily, and rushed out, feeling as if she'd burst into tears at any moment.

Yet she didn't cry, once she'd reached the safety of her room. Instead she sat by the open window and stared out into the moonlit garden, her mind suspended in frozen desolation while the hours ticked by. Her heart was thudding as she waited, dreading a knock on the door that meant Luciano was coming to fulfil his one-time threat to seduce her.

Two o'clock. Her bones felt stiff and her flesh chilled. He wasn't coming to batter the door down after all. Was she glad or sorry? She sighed. Who the hell knew what went on in her jumble of a brain any more?

And then she saw him, his dark head and the white dinner-jacket immediately recognisable as he strolled into the garden. Afraid of moving in case he saw her, she watched as he paused in the middle of the path and stood as still as a statue for some time. Her eyes devoured him and her heart went out to him.

'Luciano, Luciano, Luciano,' she whispered, savouring his name.

His head lifted as if he'd heard her and he turned, his whole body energised, it seemed. His dark eyes unerringly sought her room. Debbie stopped breathing. 'Debbie,' he said softly. 'How beautiful you are.'

She groaned, inhaling the scent of a thousand roses, and found herself incapable of moving. With his eyes fixed steadily on hers, he walked to the wisteria that scrambled all over the cloister roof and began to climb.

Her hands trembled in sheer panic because it was clear from the determined expression on his face that he was on his way to force her to surrender herself to him.

'Go back,' she pleaded. 'Don't do it. You'll ruin my good memories of you.'

Frantically she fumbled for the catch to release the shutters. Too late. He had his hand on the sill, was leaping into the room...

'Debbie!' he said urgently.

'No,' she cried in distress, her eyes a pale silver with dismay. 'Don't, Luciano, don't!'

'I must!' he said, advancing relentlessly.

'No——'

'I have to!' he growled roughly.

He caught her by the shoulders and through the thinness of her cotton nightdress she felt the difference in their body temperatures. She was as cold as ice, he as hot as a furnace.

'Why?' she asked brokenly.

His mouth descended on hers. 'Because of that,' he whispered, and kissed her again. 'And that.'

She wanted to stop him—she really did. But her body wouldn't join in with her brain and fight him. Her arms wound around his neck and she found herself kissing him back, drowning in the sensual delight of his tender lips, urging him to take away the ache in her heart and the hunger in her soul.

And then, to her utter dismay, he was pushing her back. 'I must leave,' he said thickly.

Debbie blinked, uncomprehending. 'L-leave?' she squeaked.

He looked at her sternly. 'Leave.'

Her nerves were in rags. With a rasping breath that skittered through her tense, hungry body, she said, 'You—you're not going to...seduce me?'

'Hell, Debbie!' he grated.

'I don't understand,' she whispered.

'You will; I promise you you will. I can't stay a second longer.'

'You—you don't want me?' she gulped.

'Don't stop me!' he growled. 'Don't say anything!'

He walked to the locked door and turned the key, then opened the door while Debbie watched in amazement. He meant to go. He was going! Stunned, she heard him run down the stairs and then, a little later, she heard a car start up and drive away. He'd gone!

He'd gone to all the effort of climbing up to her room...for what? A kiss? She touched her soft lips, thinking of the kiss and how she had known it would be that wonderful. But not for him, apparently. She didn't match up to his expectations.

She scowled at herself in the mirror. He'd tried her and obviously found her wanting, so she might as well stop moping and get some sleep. Things to do tomorrow. Cracked hearts to seal over.

Wearily she dragged herself to bed. Dawn wasn't far off and it was going to be a long day. She squeezed her eyes tightly shut. A long lifetime without Luciano. She would have her son and her family, but she wanted Luciano too. She wanted it all—and she knew life wasn't that generous.

'Get used to it,' she said aloud, then sighed in resignation. 'You've got more than most.' She spent the rest of the night awake, reliving every conversation, every glance, every touch. It was sweet torture but she had to do it.

In the morning, she mechanically got Stefano ready for travelling and took him down to breakfast. Luciano wasn't there—but Pia was, fiddling impatiently with a silver coffee-pot. Debbie eyed her wearily, knowing she spelt trouble.

'You're leaving, then. He persuaded you,' said Pia.

'Yes.'

'You look exhausted. Did he sleep with you?' she asked rudely.

Debbie glared and listlessly strapped Stefano in the high chair that Enrico had supplied. 'No.'

'Oh. He didn't fancy you, then. I suppose,' she said nastily, 'he must have gone off to that woman who had his brat.'

Debbie froze. That wasn't some idle comment. She remembered that Luciano had driven off last night. Why did anyone ever drive somewhere in the early hours?

'What woman?' she asked as casually as her dry throat would allow her.

'Oh, they've been together for years,' Pia said scathingly. 'Don't you pick up any gossip? He must have been ... oh, eighteen when he fathered her bastard. A girl.'

'Luciano ... a father? He has a mistress?' Debbie choked.

'She used to be a maid,' said Pia, pouring herself a cup of coffee. 'Why do you think the villagers dislike him? They know the trouble he caused the family. And he had the nerve to blame Gio! Talk about a coward!' she said scornfully.

'Oh, God!' whispered Debbie. He was as bad as his brother. Out of the same mould.

'Toast, please!' demanded Stefano, banging his spoon on the tray in front of him.

'Toast.' Automatically, Debbie buttered a round and cut it up into triangles.

'I came to make sure you knew.' Pia's eyes narrowed. 'He'll want to install the woman and his brat. Gio's mother and I think that you should let your kid stay and stop Luciano from taking over here.'

'I couldn't,' said Debbie with a shudder. 'Not now.'

'You must!' Pia hissed furiously. 'Luciano will ruin everything! The family relies on the income from the estate to live on.'

'Luciano won't stop them working, surely?' frowned Debbie.

'Working? They don't *work*,' Pia said in horror.

Debbie gave her a direct look and remembered how Luciano had said the family had been draining the estate dry. 'Then it's time they did,' she muttered grimly.

Pia stopped and listened. Debbie, too, could hear the sound of a car approaching. 'Hell! It's him! I'm going. Leave that brat here,' was her parting shot. 'That'll take the smile off Luciano's smug face!'

Debbie sank into a chair. Luciano, like his father, had a long-term mistress. He was spoken for. She heaved a deep sigh. That explained why he'd been aroused by her and yet had held back. He'd responded as a normal healthy male would, but his heart lay elsewhere and he'd gone to the woman he loved for the night.

'Sarno!' crowed Stefano in delight. Debbie didn't turn round. She felt too miserable. 'Gum-ma!' squealed Steffy.

'Grandma isn't here, sweetheart,' she said heavily.

'Grandma certainly is!' came her mother's voice.

She whipped her head around and stared stupidly. Luciano—with... 'Mother?' she gasped.

'Gum-ma!' squealed Steffy again.

'Oh, Mum, Mum, Mum!' She ran to her mother and flung herself into the wonderfully loving arms.

'Darling Debs,' said her mother affectionately, hugging her very, very tightly. 'You are a fool. Hello, poppet.'

Completely confused, Debbie watched her mother lift Stefano from the chair and cuddle him. 'You... How...? I... Why on earth have you come?' she asked her mother in amazement. 'And how? I was going home...'

'So I hear,' said her mother, vigorously buttering another slice of toast for Stefano with one hand and jiggling him on her hip at the same time. 'Isn't that extraordinary? I thought you were hanging on for a few days. When Luciano rang last night and said he had some business to talk over with me——'

'But Mother, you won't be working any longer,' Debbie cut in, mystified. 'And who's managing the business at the moment?'

'The most amazing troupe of people you've ever clapped eyes on,' said her mother calmly. 'So don't worry about it. Me, I'm going to enjoy my fortnight here.'

'F-fortnight?' Debbie gaped in horror.

'And you'll stay too, to make sure your mother's all right. Won't you?' Luciano smiled innocently.

'I—I can't,' she said in dismay. 'Luciano, you know I'm taking Steffy home today.'

'Oh, no. I don't think Luciano would have let you do that, love,' her mother demurred.

'What?'

'He wants you to stay——'

'No, he doesn't!' Debbie yelled in frustration.

'I do.' Luciano's eyes smouldered. 'Oh, Debbie, you've no idea how much I do.'

'He's been hit by a lightning bolt,' grinned her mother.

'Oh-h-h,' Debbie groaned in anguish, blushing to the roots of her hair when she realised what her mother was suggesting. 'How can you say such a thing?'

'Because it's true,' she soothed. 'And from what I hear you've been hit by a lightning bolt too, and you don't argue with nature. When it hits, it hits. And there's nothing you can do about it.'

'I'm sorry about this, Luciano,' mumbled Debbie, deeply embarrassed by her mother's mistake. 'You've got the wrong end of the stick, Mum! I don't know why or how you got here...'

'Luciano phoned me up in the middle of the night and persuaded me to come over. He's very persuasive,' grinned her mother. 'We talked for ages over breakfast in Palermo and then we drove here. I'm dead beat. How about a cup of tea?'

'Tea? *Tea*?' cried Debbie hysterically. 'Luciano! What's going on?'

'Don't you know? Are you really that blind?' he teased gently. 'I'm trying to make you see that I adore you, love you——'

'Love!' The lie sliced her heart in two. 'Don't you start! You love your mistress.'

'Who? Are you crazy?' He grinned. 'Jealousy! I like it. Don't worry, sweetheart, I don't have a mistress.'

'Don't "sweetheart" me,' she cried frantically. 'Pia said——'

'Ah, Pia,' he cut in, a flash of anger in his dark eyes. 'I suggest you talk to the staff if you want the truth. I imagine she's told you about the woman I've been supporting for the last ten years.'

'Yes! And your daughter!' she blazed.

Luciano's eyes danced. 'Such jealousy! That's very promising,' he purred. 'Listen, Debbie, neither has ever been mine. They were Gio's. When Gio got the maid pregnant, she was given a house and told to keep her mouth shut. But there was gossip and suspicion which fell on me; Gio fanned the flames, I think,' he said cynically.

'Shocking!' declared her mother.

'It was convenient for everyone to blame me,' said Luciano with a shrug. 'Unfortunately, I refused to take the blame and the villagers shunned me from that moment on, believing me to be a man without honour. I think you'll find that the maid is now putting the record straight. I took her under my protection to prevent anyone harming her or tormenting her child. I know what it's like to be a bastard in a hostile environment, you see.'

'Oh.' Debbie felt shocked. But she knew from the way he'd spoken that it was true and Pia's tale had been a tissue of lies. 'I made a mistake. I'm sorry I doubted you,' she said quietly and shyly she lifted her eyes to his. He'd said he loved her. Dared she believe *that*?

'Steffy and me are going to feed toast to the ducks,' her mother announced, sniffing into a handkerchief and scooping up a buttery Stefano hastily. She disappeared through the doorway and could be heard chatting happily as she trotted down the path.

Debbie lowered her eyes in embarrassment at the sudden silence that fell.

'Look at me,' commanded Luciano gently. 'Look at me.'

She lifted her lashes and was transfixed by the tenderness in his eyes. 'Oh, Luciano,' she faltered.

'I do love you,' he said softly, coming to take her in his arms. 'I've loved you for a long time. I thought I could let you go, but I found it impossible. I nearly persuaded myself that it would be for the best. And I almost broke my heart, having to send you away.'

'But—but last night...' she stammered. 'You didn't...'

'Last night I wanted to make love to you very, very badly. It was a terrible effort to content myself with just a kiss,' he said roughly. 'I knew I'd be tempted by you if I stayed. We'd become lovers.' He groaned. 'It was agony! You were so suspicious and uncertain and the only way I could convince you I was serious was to show you how much I respect you.'

'Respect!' she cried in astonishment.

'Of course,' he said gravely. 'An honourable man doesn't treat the woman he loves, the woman he intends to marry, with disrespect.'

'Luciano,' she breathed. 'Why... why...?'

'Poor darling,' he murmured, nuzzling her ear. 'You've no idea how close I was to throwing all my principles out of the window and surrendering to you. You're unfairly irresistible to me,' he said thickly.

'I am?' she quavered.

'Can't you feel?' he growled. 'How I shake when you're near? How my eyes soften with desire, with love and longing?'

'I—I thought it was my imagination—that you couldn't possibly——'

'Well, I can and I do,' he muttered hoarsely, his body tense against hers. 'Last night you told me you hadn't loved Gio and you seemed unhappy about leaving. I knew I had a chance. Our physical attraction had become clear very early on, but love takes time. And I wanted time.' He smiled into her wide eyes. 'I knew I'd find it hard, waiting for you to recognise my love. So I thought I'd better find a chaperon who'd be sympathetic to my cause.'

'My mother!' Debbie laughed. He was afraid of his need for her! And he loved her. Joy burst into her heart. He loved her!

'Yes.' He gave her a pained look. 'I'm going to need someone very strict to keep me from your room, your bed, your beautiful, beautiful body.'

His hand caressed her hair, his eyes full of love, and Debbie's heart opened like a flower. 'I love you so much,' he said huskily. 'So very much. I hope in time you will be my wife. But I have no intention of making love to you until our wedding-day.

'Debbie,' he went on passionately, 'I have spent my whole life searching for you, waiting for the bolt to hit me. And then, when I least expected—or wanted—it, you rolled into my office and into my life! Funny, courageous—and my brother's wife. It felt as if someone had smashed a brick between my eyes. I could hardly concentrate for wanting to leap over my desk and declare what had happened.'

'Luciano!' she said in delight. 'How wicked!'

'I was so angry,' he said with a rueful grin. 'You aroused me so fast and I couldn't understand how I could lose control so alarmingly. Work is work! So I tried to get rid of you. But when you spotted the photograph you looked so shocked and my heart went out to you. I felt compelled to take you home.'

'And you came later, to tell me about Gio,' she remembered.

He kissed the lines which had gathered on her forehead. 'I had to. I didn't want you to worry when he didn't come home. I longed to see you again but I thought you loved him, and I couldn't bear to think of you finding out about Gio's failings. So I contented myself with hearing your voice on the phone.'

'You cared, you really cared, all that time ago?' she said shakily, stunned by his unselfishness.

'All the time,' he said, a catch in his husky voice. 'Which is why I didn't want you to come here, if you remember. When you turned up here with Stefano, I was horrified because you'd obviously find out some things you'd rather not know. I wanted to shake you.' He groaned at the memory. 'And I was torn between encouraging you to stay and——'

'Using all your persuasive powers to make me go home,' she finished wryly.

He nodded. 'I only wanted what would be best for you,' he murmured into her hair. His hands caressed her shoulders. 'I imagined you were mourning my brother. I hated him then! I was jealous—jealous that he'd known you. And now I know what a blind fool he was, because he never recognised your qualities.'

'You said I was blind,' she remembered, leaning into his chest.

'I thought everyone must be able to see what I felt about you,' he chuckled. 'It was hard, denying myself what I wanted—you, Steffy and the estate. How could I ever hope to have such riches land in my lap? And I truly believed that you had too much to lose in England and it would be better for you to go home.'

'You changed your mind,' she said softly.

He gave a satisfied sigh. 'Yes, thank God! I'm afraid I deceived you. I pretended that there wasn't a flight,' he said, a twinkle in his dark eyes.

'But you didn't tell me how you felt,' she protested.

He kissed her sulky mouth and turned it into a smile. 'Because you had to realise what *you* felt first. You had to admit it to yourself. I knew you would. You were teetering on the brink and by making our parting very real to you I pushed you over.'

Her mouth trembled. Tears of happiness ran down her cheeks and he kissed her eyes gently. 'Manipulator,' she mumbled. 'I went through hell.'

'And you'll find heaven, if I have my way. I want to care for you, Debbie. Love you, cherish you. I want to look after you—you and Steffy and your mother—all my life,' he murmured passionately.

'Oh, Luciano, I love you so much,' she said tremulously. He kissed her and she melted deeper into his arms, delirious with happiness.

'Gently,' he said, moving her away a little. 'Remember my passion. I have to hold it in check. That's why your mother is here. We will be very circumspect. You and your mother and Steffy will live here and you will sometimes ask me to visit you, from one of the estate cottages where I'll be staying.'

'Anything!' she cried fervently. 'Anything, if I can be with you. I love you, Luciano!' She lifted her mouth to his and grew dizzy with his kisses. It would be hard, terribly hard, waiting for their wedding-day. But it would be worth the wait.

*   *   *

Six months later she was in Luciano's arms again—but this time it was her wedding-day. All of her family were there, plus the house staff, the villagers and people from his bank in Palermo where he was now based. Some of the Colleoni, too, who'd made their peace and their apologies to Luciano.

Even Gio's mother. It hadn't been easy, getting her to see that Luciano had hardly been responsible for the circumstances of his birth. But Debbie had gently pointed out that Stefano was innocent of *his* circumstances and Gio's mother had gradually been won round because she idolised Steffy.

Time had healed the wounds and today Luciano had been able to hug Gio's mother and accept her good wishes for their happiness. Thinking of that moment, Debbie felt tears of joy spring into her eyes. The wait had been hard, but Luciano's patience had been rewarded.

Over the months, she had fallen deeper and deeper in love with him. She smiled to think of the sweet way he played with Steffy and how he was helping her to bring up her son with great humour and firmness. And how much joy he'd brought into her mother's life, how tender, caring and courteous he was.

'Just like your dad,' her mother had said, and that had been the greatest compliment of all.

She sighed happily. 'Christmas in London,' she said to Luciano, wiping a piece of wedding-cake from the corner of his mouth. 'Won't it be lovely?'

'I'm looking forward to it,' he said fondly. 'And to bringing your entire family over here next spring. It'll be one humdinger of a party!' His eyes kindled as he studied her rapt face. 'How I love you,' he said huskily. 'I think it's time we slipped away. Mmm?'

She nodded.

And in the soft, velvety darkness of an island in the Pacific they consummated their love. Some time late in the night a tropical storm broke out over their heads and they both laughed and cried out, 'Lightning bolts!'

Still giggling, Debbie snuggled into Luciano's strong arms. 'I'm so happy,' she confided contentedly.

'Me too.' His lips were tender on hers. 'And I'll love you forever, my darling. You know that, don't you?'

'Yes!' Unable to speak further for emotion, she gave him a radiant smile instead which told him all he needed to know. The storm seemed to fade into the distance. Her mind, her body, her heart and soul were filled with a feeling of sheer joy as she began to return his kisses. And she knew that her happiness was lasting, because they had both finally found true love.

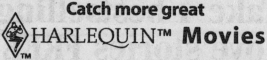

Take 4 bestselling love stories FREE

Plus get a FREE surprise gift!

She's a woman without a future
because of her past.

THE
DAUGHTER

At fifteen, Maggie is convicted of her mother's
murder. Seven years later she escapes from
prison to prove her innocence.

After many years on the run, Maggie makes a
dangerous decision: to trust Sean McLeod, the cop she
has fallen in love with. She knows he can do one of two
things: he can turn her in or help her find her mother's
real killer. She feels her future is worth the risk....

JASMINE
CRESSWELL

Available in April 1998 at your favorite retail outlet.

MJC425